Billionaire Promise

J.L. Ryan

Published by J.L. Ryan, 2018.

This is a work of fiction. Similarities to real people, places, or events are entirely coincidental.

BILLIONAIRE PROMISE

First edition. June 17, 2018.

ISBN: 978-1386637219

Written by J.L. Ryan.

The Billionaire Boss

There had to be something she could do, but what? Plus-size Rachel Greene looked at her surroundings and sighed. She jumped at the chance to live on her own, but now, she was in over her head. She had always been the one who wanted out. Out of the family, out of the drama, out of everything, and now, she was stuck in a tiny apartment in the worst neighborhood in D.C., with no hope of changing it. She put her head in her hands and sighed. On the computer screen in front of her, was her budget for the next six months. No matter which way she plotted and planned, she only had about two months before it all fell apart. She leaned back in her seat, glancing at her ample reflection in the mirror on her desk.

She wasn't gorgeous by any means, at least not in her opinion. She was studious and bookwormy, and very curvy. At least that's what her friends used to call her. She had long chestnut hair, blue eyes, and long eyelashes, which was something her grandmother said was a wonderful asset. She wore glasses most of the time unless she had some special occasion, then she popped in her contacts. She was well-built and rubenesque, something else her grandmother said was a good thing. Not that it mattered because at 24 she had been to school most of her life and still, there was nothing to show for it. Sure, she could go home if things got too bad. The problem was, she would rather live in her car first.

She loved her family, there was no denying that. She was the oldest, with a younger brother who was 20. He decided to start his adult life much earlier and was married with a three-year-old daughter, and a baby on the way. He also lived at home with their parents and grandmother, and his wife. When Tim started his new life, Rachel started hers. At first, her mother was sad she was moving out, but it was only a week before they moved the kids into her old room. There was something co-dependent about her family that made her want

1

out. Everything they did, they did as one cohesive unit, no opinions required. Everything was about survival and scraping along, something Rachel was fine doing, but she would just as soon do it alone, without the heavy responsibility of six other people.

She looked back down at the screen. It wasn't doing much good right now, living her own life. She graduated from the local community college with a degree in Office Management. Somehow, her family talked her into getting student loans along the way so that she could "help out" with the extra money. Now she was in debt, with payments that were ridiculous and despite her efforts, she couldn't seem to find a job anywhere. If she'd only been able to keep her job at the hospital none of this would be happening! Even thinking about it made her skin crawl. She was good at her job there, always on time, and working harder than most. She wasn't tooting her own horn so to speak, it simply was the fact of the matter. One would think her dedication to the job would be something to applaud, but in truth it did nothing more but put her in a vulnerable situation where dirty old men could hit on her. Not just any dirty old man either. Dr. Peter Evans was her superior, she would even say that initially she liked him. It wasn't until he cornered her in a supply room groping at her that she felt disgust more than anything.

He was old enough to be her father yet he claimed that she was giving him mixed signals, which she strongly denied. He begged her not to say anything, and she didn't. If for any other reason than the fact that his career would be over if she did, and part of her believed he truly though she was into him. Every point he made was true. She came early and stayed late. She always turned in things to him personally. In her mind this was the action of a good employee, not someone looking for a good time from her boss. Either way, she now was very careful about what she did and how. The problem was after she left the hospital, she couldn't find work anywhere. At first she told herself it would just take a little longer. But now, three weeks later, she was concerned. She leaned back in the chair and bit her thumbnail lost in thought. She didn't want to wreak havoc on her family, she certainly didn't want to sleep on a couch while paying for storage. She leaned forward again and jumped into a new job search, hopeful something would happen.

Byron Blakemore was tired and aching. He spent the early morning hours at the gym, hoping to relieve some of the stress he was carrying around, but looking across his desk he felt the familiar tension rise up. Some days he wondered what the hell he was paying these people for at all. He buzzed in Linda, who scurried in, pen and pad in hand.

"Yes Mr. Blakemore?" She was a small lady. Probably no more than 4'9 and pushing 60. He knew she was struggling more and more to do her job, but he didn't have the heart to let her go.

"Linda, can you set up a meeting with Carlisle please? Also, I need something purchased for my mother's birthday, I thought you might like the task." He saw her light up and he smiled to himself, Shopping seemed to be a skill most women mastered at, and retained an entire lifetime.

"Yes, Mr. Blakemore." She scurried towards his door.

"Oh Linda, one more thing can you send Alice in HR up for me. We need to discuss something."

At her nod, he dove back into his paperwork. There was always something that needed his attention, but this was too much. He leaned back once more rethinking the board of directors. There was no fire from any of them to make this business grow. He would be lying if he said he didn't enjoy the money, he did. He'd grown accustom to a certain kind of lifestyle and he wasn't about to give it up. He knew he had a reputation of being a stone-faced ass, but he preferred it that way, less drama. The only person who really knew him was his mother. She was a sweet woman and anyone who thought otherwise was a fool. He was worried about her, she was frail now and needed more than just he could provide. He heard the knock at his door.

"Yes, come in." It was Alice.

She walked into the room and pushed the door shut quietly locking it, before she walked over to his desk. She gave him a smile and he stood up, buttoning his jacket as he went. He walked towards her and tucked an arm around her waist, pulling her to him in a crushing kiss. She was the kind of tension relief he needed. He nibbled at her neck.

"I'm glad you're here today Alice, I'd hate to have to write you up for being absent again." He growled into her neck as she tilted back her head, enjoying his every move.

"You know very well why I was late on Monday, Mr. Blakemore." She moved to pull off her top and he gingerly kissed the tops of her breasts when his phone rang. He decided to ignore it and continue on until they were both naked.

She moved with precision as she worked her way down his body. There was something nice about how she took charge, not making him work for it. It was a mutual understanding the two of them shared. Both needing something, and eager to help the other. Even now as she moved her mouth down his body he relaxed. He always enjoyed the talent she had at making things happen quickly and today was no different. He stopped her, pulling her up the length of him and moving to lay her on the desk. She smiled up at him greedily licking her lips as he pushed into her, filling her and owning her in that moment. It was over quickly, both finding a need fulfilled and both happy with the arrangement. Alice, after all, had a husband she didn't love, who consistently cheated on her with numerous woman in the building. He was actually working in accounting upstairs, clueless to the fact that his wife had not only found out his secrets, but was taking some pleasure out of life herself. It was how they started up, he told her about her husband. Not intentionally, but in passing, not knowing she was his wife at first. When she demanded to know more he showed her the footage caught on surveillance. Normally not talked to with any sort of demanding tone she amused him, and so the affair began.

Neither of them had any thoughts about it leading to anything. She was far too uncaring about the world, or the business. She amused him and met his needs sexually, but nothing more. Never having one serious conversation together before it was clear this was a temporary thing for them both. She was something to play with and he made sure she enjoyed it. He watched her button and fix her blouse in an effort to appear normal once more. Even that made him smile, he knew she would be reliving it for hours.

She turned to look at him. "Linda said you need me." All business now she sat across from him waiting to hear what he needed her to do.

"Yes, I need you to look into finding someone for me, for my mother actually. She is independent enough, but I worry for her. Someone not necessarily a nurse who wants to do everything for her, more of a companion."

"I can look into a few places, sure." She stood to leave. "When do you want them?"

"Let' shoot for next week, set up some interviews, I want to have a direct hand in finding the right person." He gave her a smile as he went back to work. "Have a good day Alice." He watched a smile cross her face and her exit.

A week later, Rachel found herself in the lobby of the Blakemore. She was surprised, she actually had been one of the people called in to interview for a position she wasn't even remotely qualified for. Blakemore was a large corporation and one she was always reading about or hearing on the news. She looked down at her hands nervously, she could only hope she wouldn't get thrown out right away. Why would someone looking for a companion be interviewing at Blakemore? Whatever the reason she was happy to be there. She looked around her at the other people waiting. Some in scrubs some in designer jackets. She pulled on her skirt, self-conscious about herself more now than before. It was obvious she didn't fit in, but this was her only chance to stay put, in her own place. Somehow she was going to march into the office and explain why they needed her here at Blakemore. It was a long shot, she knew it, but it was the only hand she had.

After a grueling hour she was finally next. The cute little blond who was directing everyone seemed to enjoy working here. She made her way over to look down at Rachel and she felt herself being judged, not something she ever enjoyed.

"You must be Miss Greene?" At her nod she told her to come along and follow her.

She made her way down a long corridor and finally to an office separated from the rest of the building. It was in a half moon shaped and separated by double doors which went from the secretarial area to what must be his office. She was escorted to the door where the blond pushed them open and allowed her to walk inside.

"Mr. Blakemore will be right back, just have a seat, please."
The blond left, closing one of the doors behind her, leaving Rachel to look around the room.

At first she made an effort to sit down, but as she looked at the city below she couldn't help but walk over to the windows. There were only two walls in the entire office, both of those attached to the double doors facing inward. The rest of the office was in a half circle facing the city and the walls were floor to ceiling windows looking out. From where she stood it almost felt like flying. It was beautiful, she always loved the city, and although living as close as a child in Virginia she rarely made it to D.C. to see the sights. Once she went to a field trip with school and she was overwhelmed by the history, as well as the things you could see in the museums. Even now she smiled as she got as close to the edge of the window as possible and looked down.

"Be careful, if you do that too long it can make you sick." She jumped back the voice scaring her.

She spun around and saw him there. He was dressed impeccably, as if the suit was molded to him. He was tall, and his face was defined by a strong jawline and the sharp planes of his face. His hair was jet blacked and slightly longer on top, but brushed back off of his forehead. Despite all of this it was his eyes that held her the longest. They were a deep blue, and piercing. It felt as though he was looking into her soul.

"I'm so sorry, its just such a beautiful view." She smiled at him and gave her a one over. He moved to sit behind his desk and she scrambled to sit back in her chair. She watched how he moved with grace and she felt nervous now about being here under false pretenses. She took a deep breath and swallowed.

"I see you have a degree in Office Management? Is that right Miss Greene?" He looked at her, there was something slightly amusing in his tone and she cleared her throat.

"Ye... yes I do. To be honest, I was thinking the ad may have been a misprint or something?" She shrugged slightly. "When I saw the company name I thought it would be a good idea to come in, and see if perhaps it... ah well to see if it was... a misprint." She looked away and blushed. She was rambling like an idiot.

"So, you decided to come to this job interview for a position you aren't qualified for because you assumed someone was inept at posting the ad? I'm not sure if insulting the business is such a good start, Miss Greene."

"Oh no, that's not it at all, I simply wanted to come in and... will see." His voice was rising now and she felt the heat rushing to her face. This guy was obviously an ass, and rude to boot. She felt his eyes on her again looking her over.

"Tell me, Miss Greene what are you good at?" He leaned back in his chair slightly, obviously enjoying the game they were playing.

She gulped. "As you mentioned, I have a degree in Office Management. I am also good at being organized, being on time and I am a stickler for having a very determined personality."

"Very determined? Well then, that's something we have in common." He smiled as he leaned forward. "Unfortunately, the ad was correct, I am looking for a caregiver for my mother. That being said, I appreciate the time you took to come in, and I have enjoyed our discussion." He stood, buttoning his jacket.

"Well, thank you Mr.....?" She shook the hand he held out to her.

"Blakemore." He held her hand just a second longer than normal and she moved to make her way to the door. "Miss Greene..." he called out to her.

"Yes."

"If anything opens up I'll call you myself." He gave her a flash of a smiled before he sat down dismissing her.

She shut the door behind her with a slight slam. She could still feel the heat in her cheeks and she was frustrated. What a jerk, it was the only thing she could come up with off the top of her head. More importantly, what the hell was wrong with her, she usually could handle herself with some self-control and he had gotten under the skin. He would call her directly? As if somehow she should feel special. As much as she wanted to scream her frustration about the charismatic billionaire, Blakemore, she really just wanted to cry. It took a lot to bring her spirits down, and she was nearing her breaking point. She climbed into her car and sighed. At least she tried. Now, she would make the trip into Virginia for lunch with her mother, who would drill her for information about her life, or lack thereof.

Byron sighed. Finding someone who would suit his mother was proving to be a difficult challenge. Three days later and still he looked down at the stack of resumes on his desk and started sorting them one by one. Near the end he found Rachel Greene and he smiled. She was fire and ice that one. She was beautiful too, but he had a sneaking suspicion she didn't know it. She walked into his office and with a simplistic beauty looked out over the city and even then he wanted her. There was a part of him that was attracted to her innocence, the simple joy that crossed her face in those moments. Then, as the conversation began, he knew the precise moment when he frustrated her and made her angry. The crystal clear blue eyes shot daggers at him across the desk. She amused him, and excited him. He put her into the "no" pile and went on. Soon he narrowed it down to three people, all capable and seemingly nice. His mother could choose who she liked best. He buzzed Linda.

She came in with a smile and he noticed she was walking a little slower than she had that morning. He really should find her an assistant of some kind. He may very well be an ass to most, but he had a soft spot for Linda and knew her paycheck was important to her.

"Linda, I know you're busy. I wanted to ask you something, your opinion really." He walked over and sat on the corner of his desk. Linda smiled at him and sat down in the chair across from him.

"Yes Mr. Blakemore what is it, I'm happy to help however I can." She gave him a big smile and reminded him so much of his own mother he patted her arm.

"I am thinking of promoting you, to something more detailed. The problem is you will have to spend less time working with me and more time doing paperwork and such."

"Oh Mr. Blakemore, I know you let me stay because you're so sweet. I couldn't possibly get a promotion." She waved a hand at him.

"On the contrary Linda, you would be doing me a great service being in charge of some important clients. Helping me with meetings and the like. Plus, it comes with an assistant." He glanced down and removed an imaginary something from his pant leg.

"I've never had an assistant before." She gave him a wide smile. "Whatever you think is best Mr. Blakemore." She made her way back out to her desk.

After she was gone, he glanced down at the files on his desk. He knew exactly the right candidate for the new open position. He smiled to himself. He did tell her he would call her directly. She more than likely found another position by now, but the banter would be fun in and of itself. He dialed and she answered on the third ring,

"Hello!" She was noticeably out of breath making him wonder what she had been doing... or better yet, who she was doing it with.

"Miss Greene, how are you?"

"I'm fine, who is this please?" She was obviously moving something around.

"This is Mr. Blakemore... we met last week." There was a pause before she responded.

"Yes, Mr. Blakemore, how could I forget?" She said it sweetly, but he could detect a hint of sarcasm there. He smiled, he really did enjoy this.

"I was calling you about a position we have open, but if you're busy..."

"No! No, I'm not busy at all Mr. Blakemore, please, please go on." He felt it then, the tightness of his slacks. There was something about the way she pleaded with him that made him want her.

"I have an opening, it's a secretarial position... decent starting pay, benefits, etc. I know you mentioned you were looking."

"Yes, I am looking. I'd like to come in and discuss it, if that's ok?" She did her very best to sound nonchalant about the situation.

"Great, let's shoot for tomorrow 9 am?"

"That sounds fine with me, I don't think I have anything going on tomorrow at all." She did her very best to sound as though she may need to check.

She didn't want to appear desperate. She hung up the phone and sat down in the chair, maybe this was it but then who knew? He seemed to be genuine. She looked around the room at the boxes she was currently packing. As much as she tried to deny it, there was no way she would miss that meeting. She had very little time before she was out on the street. She sorted through her things to find a dress she only wore on special occasions. It was tight and black. Perhaps if she tried really hard it would show, and he would be inclined to ask her to stay. She held it up in front of her and frowned. He had such an effect on her it would be hard to ignore him, but she would do her best. She fired up her computer again rearranging her numbers with her new projected income... yes, it would certainly be a blessing in disguise. She snapped it shut and went back to packing, there was a good chance she would say the wrong thing, he got under her skin and she was quick to snap at him. Something she rarely ever did. He had this uncanny way of bringing out the worst in her. She worked late, managing to eat a heated can of ravioli for dinner along the way.

The next morning came bright and sunny. She smiled as she remembered that today could change her life. She jumped out of bed and ran into the shower. It took her longer than usual to dress and apply some slight makeup before heading downtown. There was a hustle and bustle in the air as she rode along, mindful of the people in the crosswalks and those begging for loose change. This was home and she loved it. She pulled into the parking garage and crossed her fingers that he would validate her parking ticket. She didn't even have enough money to get out of here if he didn't. She took a deep breath as the elevator took her to the top floor. When the doors opened, she made her way to the front desk and waited. Soon a short smiling lady who resembled her grandmother came to get her.

> "You must be Rachel, come on dear, let me show you around." She was slightly hunched over and moving at a slow pace and Rachel loved her instantly. "Mr. Blakemore wants to meet with you for lunch, but until then I'm going to show you around a bit. He says he is "promoting" me." She gave the bunny ears as she explained. "The truth is I am old and need to retire but I would be lost all alone at home, and he knows it. So he is hiring my replacement, with the title of being my assistant." She gave a chuckle and they moved towards her office.

Although she had been through these rooms before, and back to his private office, she wasn't prepared for the size of the actual space she would be working in. Directly in front of his double doors was a lounge area, for meetings and to one side a fully stocked guest kitchen, the other entire wall was made for his assistant. She hadn't expected it to be quite so beautiful, really. She refused to get her hopes up, but she knew it would be difficult. Linda, she learned, was showing her where her desk was, as well as her private office behind it. At her confused look Linda explained.

"Sometimes, Mr. Blakemore has guests come over and they will sit out there in the lounge drinking and talking. Sometimes about the most ridiculous of things, you know how men are. This office in the back is yours for your personal use really, When you can do extra paperwork, etc., away from the hubbub."

Linda pushed open the door to the office space and Rachel was stunned. It was bigger than her entire apartment and was complete with a small kitchen of its own, a bathroom and a small sitting area. It was decorated in hues of pink and white and had a window of its own also, floor to ceiling but not nearly as wide. The idea of not getting her hopes tossed out the window by now and she spun around to see Linda's smiling face.

"Wow, it certainly is something Miss Linda isn't it?" She gave her a smile.

"Yes, it is and you will enjoy it, I can assure you. Come sit down with me." Linda walked over to the intercom system and buzzed.

"Yes, this is Linda, can you have a switchboard redirect Mr. Blakemore's calls for the interim. I'll let you know when I am back. "After a pause, she added.' Thank you Mary." She hung up and made her way back to the small sofa in the room. She settled in and Rachel was amused at the say she kicked off her shoes and leaned back to relax.

"I am most certainly getting old, my dear. Now let's talk turkey. Off of that main kitchen across the way there is another office much like this one but a little smaller. It's not connected to Mr. Blakemore's office like this one." She pointed to a seam in the door that she hadn't seen before. "I plan on setting up myself over there. I don't need as much space since I'll be passing off the bigger things to you. As a matter of fact, I've already moved over there and have yet to tell Byron." She gave her a smile.

"Byron?" Rachel was doing her best to follow along, but it was proving difficult.

"Mr. Blakemore, I used to call him Byron, but... well people thought since we were close he was showing favoritism, which he was, but then I'm old." She giggled.

Suddenly the seam in the door moved open and he was there. He gave her a once over and then smiled widely at Linda.

"I trust you have shown Rachel around some?" He offered her a hand as she tried to get up from the seat.

"I did, and she and I had an opportunity to chat some. By the way I've decided to move into the spare office behind the kitchen." She held up her hand at him. "Before you even start I did it because it suits me more, and its sound proof to all the man stuff going on in the lobby with your friends. Besides, I am thinking of cutting it down to three days a week and I don't need this much space." She said it with such finality he accepted her words without a fight.

Rachel was smiling at Linda and the match up with Byron...err...Mr. Blakemore. The two of them were like family in their banter and reminded her of her own. She watched as he delicately helped her make her way out of the room and she reevaluated her opinion of him. Maybe he wasn't a total ass after all. She waited for him to come back in and smoothed down her dress subconsciously. When she saw his shadow she stood up. He walked into the room with a smiled. He was in black today, all black and he was dashing as always. She moved her eyes back up and caught him watching her. She felt the blush rush to her face.

"Please, Miss Greene have a seat." He gestured and she did so waiting. "I hope you like what you see... of the office of course." He gave her a half smile and she felt her face turning red.

"It's lovely, very nice actually." She clasped her hands together in her lap. There was something about him that made her nervous, anxious even. Whatever it was would ultimately create a problem.

"SO you will take it, then?" He leaned forward towards her. "The job I mean." He watched her face intently.

"Don't I have to be interviewed or anything?" She frowned slightly.

"Miss Greene I think it's safe to say we have been through the interview already." He smiled at her and stood quickly, he walked over to her window.

She looked him over, him standing this way gave her a new view of him. His upper body was muscled and tight against the fabric of his suit, his body was sculpted and she knew he would be hard and muscular all over. She shook her head, trying to refocus on the task at hand.

"Then yes, I will." She stood to go, she hesitated just a moment to see what he would say next.

"We need to talk first, come in my office and shut the door behind you." He took the long strides to get there and she calmly walked behind him.

She shut the doors behind her and turned to face him. He was less than 6 inches from her. She could feel the warmth of his breath on her check and is eyes were an even deeper shade of blue. Her pulse was racing and she was both thrilled and terrified of what he would do next. She felt his hand tough her waist and the contact made her gasp slightly. He was watching her, waiting for her to move almost animalistic.

"I expect total honesty and realness between us at all times, do you understand? I also will not allow anything that goes on in this office, on any floor to be discussed outside of the office." He took a step towards her and she backed up.

"What do you mean exactly Mr. Blakemore?" She whispered the words waiting for his response.

"For example, if I have a woman here, it doesn't leave this office, if I have clients over here... nothing we talk about can be repeated. We often discuss business mergers that could make or break us."

"I understand." She swallowed hard. He was so close she could smell his aftershave and she was terrified to look into his face. She knew she would likely fall to the ground if she did the way her knees were shaking.

"Do you? What if I were to tell you that I want to kiss you. Would you feel like that is something you need to share?" He moved so that his lips were hovering just slightly above hers.

"No, not at all." She smiled at him, a new sense of confidence racing through her. He wanted to sleep with her. He didn't give one care about anything else. Just knowing it made her relax, she had dealt with co-worker issues like this before.

He watched the light flicker in her eyes and then dim. Something he said killed the kindling he was trying to ignite. He would have to figure that out, one day. "Good." He let her go and she walked towards the front door.

"Oh, and Miss Greene... I'll see you in the morning." He went back to the task at hand and she sprinted from his office.

All men were dogs, she thought. It was as simple as that, everyone she had ever met anyway. So her new boss wanted to have his way with her, big deal. Nine out of ten times it was too much time on their hands and not enough sense to put it all away, and keep it to themselves. Blakemore was a jerk just like the good doctor at the hospital. This time, however, she would call his bluff. She refused to lose her job over it this time and decided that if he did make a move, she would let it go long enough to give him enough rope to hang himself. He more than likely loved the chase the most so she wouldn't even give him one. She would be ready and willing to entertain his ideas and thoughts, but that's as far as she would let it go before putting a stop to the whole thing.

Byron sipped at the drink in his hand. What was he thinking, talking to her like that anyway? She looked like she was going to faint, and all he could think about was pushing her back on the desk and tasting her mouth. He always had some self-control and yet when she left, he'd been panting like a teenage school boy watching her leave. What was it that had her under his skin? She was beautiful, but in a nontraditional kind of way. She hadn't been prancing around the office in anything revealing like Alice typically did. It was her shyness, the way she turned away from him and refused to give in. Just thinking about her leaving and not giving in to him made her so much more challenging. His time with her would come, there was no doubt. She was like a little lamb though, he would have to be gentle with her... if he could only get himself under control.

The rest of the evening went by quickly for her as she prepared for her first day. She left her things packed, just in case. She would play this game with him, but she didn't want to lose, and she wanted to keep her job. Once she had him under her thumb she would be set, at least for a while. She could maybe get a nicer place. Plus, he did something crazy to her and she wanted to know why. Whatever happened, she would be as prepared as she could be. She moved her things around and put together a few nicer outfits. One day she would be out of this mess. She sighed as she heard the knob on her apartment door turning. Someone was always thinking this was A4. She was getting to a point where she didn't feel safe anymore. She simply had to get in good with Blakemore, then she could let him go.

The morning came and she was set to leave. She found the keys to her car and easily went out to go. In the mornings in her complex no one was awake until noon, so she was fairly safe. The evenings were something altogether different. One of her friends often told her to buy a gun, but she was absolutely against the idea. She made her way downtown and found HR, and the leggy blonde who had directed her to Blakemore's office a couple of weeks ago.

> "SO Miss Greene, you must have left quite the impression on Blakemore." She looked her over and then shrugged. "Fill out all of this stuff, then you can go upstairs."

There was obviously something about this situation that pushed blondie in a bad direction. Whatever it was had nothing to do with her, but still she felt like she had disliked her immediately. She made her way through the mountain of paperwork and was finally finished around lunchtime. She made her way to her new office and only managed to get lost once, which was something of a personal accomplishment. She unloaded her things in the back office and made her way up front. Linda was nowhere to be found so she waited. Finally, he came in.

"Linda is out sick, come sit with me today. I can have you take some notes." He moved towards his office and she followed closely behind.

He turned and shed his jacket off and she watched his movements from hooded lashes. This was going to be harder than she thought. He rolled up his sleeves and finally sat down. He gathered up some paperwork and handed it to her, not really looking at her at all and she realized she may have been completely off in her assumption of what he wanted. She frowned, her plan would never work if she didn't at least attract him at all. She went over the paperwork in hand as he started going through the merger of two small companies that was on the horizon and she listened closely, learning the lingo about how he did things. Finally an hour later he seemed to relax some.

"Sorry, I tend to get overzealous when I'm talking shop." He gave her a lazy smile, which she returned and batted her eyelashes at him.

He felt something deep down, jump at her actions. She was openly flirting with him, a leap from yesterday's declaration. Perhaps she's had a change of heart, or she was playing with him. He smiled as he thought about it. Surely she knew better than to even try, he would have her naked and on all fours in an hour if he wanted too, but she didn't know him like that yet. He decided to test the water.

"DO you have a boyfriend, Rachel?" She watched his eyes moving over her as he talked. She took a deep breath in.

"No, do you?" She gave him a half smile and he chuckled.

"No, nor do I have a wife or a girlfriend. DO you have someone... close, someone who meets your needs?" He heard her gulp and inwardly he knew he had scored the first point.

"No, there is nothing I can't do better and more efficiently myself." She stared at him hard and saw his easy smile slip slightly. "What about you Mr. Blakemore?"

"Yes." He gritted the words out. She had planted the image of herself naked and alone and it was burned into his brain. She blushed at his response, some part of her expected him to lie.

"I see, she licked her lips slightly, suddenly feeling out of control of the conversation.

"Yes, I have someone, and yes, I think I could do it more efficiently." He watched her waiting for a reaction.

"I suppose that remains to be seen, doesn't it." She stood ready to make her way back out to her office. She knew he was there before she felt his hand on her arm spinning her around. He pressed her up against the wall of the office and leaned into her. She felt his mouth crush into hers in one fell swoop. It was a demanding kiss, pressing and pushing. His hands moved against her back, pulling her closer and moving upwards until his hands were in her hair cupping her head. He moved her mouth against his, nibbling and kissing until he was recklessly kissing her deeper again. Finally, they stopped and were both panting.

"I know this game Rachel, trust me, you won't win sweetheart." He whispered it in her earlobe nipping at the earlobe. She pushed him off and straightened her clothes.

"Perhaps, I guess that too remains to be seen. You certainly have a lot to live up to Blakemore."

She moved into her office, shutting the door firmly and locking it from her side. She made her way to the desk with shaky legs and practically fell into the seat. This was not at all going the way she had planned. She was going to be firm and alluring and yet here she was a shaky mess, having five minutes ago been ready to throw herself at him. She leaned forward, her head in her hands. She had certainly put herself in a unique situation this time. The rest of the day went quickly. She spent the remainder of the afternoon navigating the computer software system. She finally left as it was nearing 6. He's made no effort to bother her the rest of the day and she eventually relaxed. She pulled up to her apartment and sighed. This was the peak time for bad things around here. She saw a group of people, mostly men gathered around the step of her building. With careful and calculated steps she maneuvered around them, despite the calls and innuendos thrown at her. She slammed the door shut behind her and she cried. Life had to get better. She would be up the rest of the night, listening for someone to come to her door as they promised to do.

The first week went by smoothly, they would run into each other on occasion and there would always be something looming between them. He didn't try to kiss her again, but he was clear in telling her he wanted to. More than once he would have her come to his office and work with him on something and she knew he was watching her, testing her. With every remark he made to prove a point she would counter with one of her own setting him off into another flurry of tension. It was becoming an overwhelmingly charged game of cat and mouse with them.

The next morning was a Friday and she was happy to get out of her place. She was dragging and she did her very best to make herself look alive once she arrived. Linda fussed over her and immediately showed her how to use the email server and set up the new voicemail. They enjoyed much of the morning together and she took notes on everything. She didn't want to give him any excuse to let her go. He finally found them at lunch and offered to take them both out which Linda happily agreed to. She could find no excuse to say no and she felt a shot of heat course through her as he put his hand on the small of her back helping her into the car. Lunch was a fun affair. The place they went was so overpriced, she found it almost difficult to order anything at all. Once the food arrived, she fell in love with it and understood why he came there as often as he mentioned in the car. After Linda decided to go home since she was still not "100%." She watched as he helped her to her car and they watched her leave the garage.

"Get back in the car, I want to show you something." He slid back into the seat and she followed suit.

She frowned as they took off, she never even considered telling him no... or asking where they were going. She simply did as he asked. She made a mental note to be leery of that next time. She knew there would be a nest time, they both enjoyed the game too much, and she wanted the security of being with someone who could protect her. She was in a financial mess and afraid to go home at night. He needed to learn that you cannot simply take what you want without giving back. The car pulled up to a golden building, it looked like a restaurant or a hotel but she wasn't sure. He gave his key to the valet and took her hand as he moved gracefully through the building.

"Mr. Blakemore, where are we going?" She asked him quietly.

"Just be patient... you will like it." He smiled at her and she felt that same sense of excitement he always brought out in her.

They took the elevator and kept going until they reached the top. He moved out of the elevator and pulled her behind him until they stopped in front of a door. He slid the key in it and it opened, he held it, allowing her to go inside. The walls were silk and in shades of gold. The farthest wall away was glass looking down and out over the city, even higher than his building did. In front of the wall was a bed, huge and waiting. She spun around to look at him. She saw him smirk and shut and lock the door behind him. She crossed her arms and waited.

"Exactly what are we doing here, Blakemore?" She took a step back as he moved towards her.

"I don't play this game with you Rachel, you want me as much as I want you, and you've told me in more ways than one. Today I'm going to make love to you, thoroughly on that bed." He spoke every word softly and dangerously as he walked towards her. She felt her hands shaking as he moved in closer.

He moved her hair back off of her shoulders and kissed the side of her exposed neck. "I know a part of you wants to make up some excuse of why we can't do this, or why it's wrong. I also know there is a part of you who wants it and needs it." He moved his hand in her hair winding it in his fist as he moved his lips over hers.

There was something frantic about their actions as they undressed each other. She couldn't form the words to tell him to stop, she was far too gone now. She felt the air rush over her exposed skin as she crawled slowly into the bed and on her back waiting for him. He waited, watching her. Naked she was even more beautiful, her skin had a healthy glow and she was curvy right down to her thighs. She was perfectly shaped for him and he wanted her more than he ever remembered wanting anyone. He made his way over to the bed. She was taking shallow breaths as he kissed her from head to toe, stopping to drink his fill of her flesh along the way. He left no inch of skin untouched by his hands and mouth.

Finally, he moved to push into her and he lost all sense of control. She fit him like a glove and it was almost painful for her. He moved slowly, gradually moving more and more until with one final push he was buried deep. He looked at her then and started moving slowly, she arched up to meet his every thrust her fingers gripping his back, her legs wrapped around his hips pulling him forwards, and deeper still. She was lost in a haze of color, feeling his moving, his touch and his mouth. She lost control of everything and dug her nails into him as she felt the explosion inside her begin to climb higher and higher until it exploded into fragmented pieces in her mind. She opened her eyes as she did it and called his name which in turn pushed him forward as well and he followed close behind. He lay there still pressed into her for a few moments until finally they moved to untangle and he found his place behind her.

No one spoke for fear of shattering the fantasy world they were both in together. She couldn't feel any sense of victory in what happened, she had no control over any of it. She was simply there, and chose to do it. Her plans to make him want her or need her somehow until he had real feelings, ones that would make him want to protect her and help her. Now, he didn't even have to buy the cow before he took what he wanted. She had never experienced anything like this before, but she knew the game was over. Her plan had failed because she was weak. Now she would never get him to notice her for anything other than this. It occurred to her that she obviously felt something more for him for it to affect her this way. She turned to move away from him, but he simply said "no" and pulled her back in close to him. She knew she would not likely find herself in this situation again and she nestled in to enjoy it for now.

Byron was lost in thought. There was something special about her, something that meant more to him than just sex. Perhaps it was the game, or the way little things made her light up. She was different, and he liked it. He knew he had won the game they were playing, but he felt no happiness in that. She tried to move away and he had stopped her. He wasn't ready yet, to face whatever happened between them. She felt good like this, in his arms. He couldn't remember ever being with a woman that he wanted to hold after sex, someone who wasn't simply there to use or be used for a natural bodily function. There was never an emotional tie to the physical act and he didn't want to start now. She needed it more than he, and he would give her that. They both napped, sleeping deeply, having been equally satisfied and content. She was the first to stir and when she noticed the clock she started to panic. She jumped up and started throwing on clothes, and he watched her.

"Was it all really that bad, that you have to run?" He gave her a half smile which she failed to respond to. He knew something wasn't right. "Rachel... are you ok."

"What... oh yes, I'm fine, I just have to get home quickly... very quickly." She was still in her panties and bra and he was enjoying the show she gave him. It wasn't long before she finally dressed the rest of the way. He stood and slid into his boxers. He watched her looking for her keys.

"Rachel... stop... your car isn't even here, calm down." He put a hand on each shoulder to calm her. He moved the hair out of her face and she looked up at him. He was standing there his bare chest, smooth under her touch and she relaxed. "Stay here with me tonight. It's already 8:30, we can have dinner and... eventually sleep." He gave her a wide smile and she smiled back.

"I don't want to be that girl... who stays too long." She screwed up her face, and he laughed.

"You're not that girl, we are just having an extended Friday afternoon that's all, nothing more."

He watched her visible slump back onto the bed. "Why do you have to get home so fast anyway?"

She swallowed, thinking of the best response. "I just like to be in before it gets too dark that's all." She smiled at him.

He frowned, he knew there was something more there, but it wasn't any of his business so he decided to let it go. He picked up the phone and ordered room service and she smiled as she looked out over the city. No matter what happened, this would be a night she would never forget.

The next day he took her to her car. She finally climbed into her bed at home at 1 in the afternoon. Part of her wanted to be happy and content with what she had been through. Another part of her wanted to cry. If she were being honest with herself, she had just been part of the most elegant and elaborate booty call ever. She should feel bad about that, but amidst all of the lovemaking they talked about life, and family. He shared his vision and hopes for the future and she, given him some version of hers. Monday she would go back to work and pretend none of it ever happened. For now she could pretend. She fell into a deep sleep, recovering from the sleep she missed the night before.

Byron was having a similar discussion with himself, he followed her home trying to see what had made her want to get back there so badly the night before. He looked up at the apartment building she entered and swore to himself. She lived here? He frowned as he looked over the streets and the neighborhood. He felt something about her situation, he wanted to get her out of here and way from the people who loitered the area. This entire block was notorious for crime and violence. He knew it was too soon to storm in there and drag her back out and into his car. He made the trek home lost in thought. He finally made his way into his penthouse, still concerned about her. What was wrong with him? He had always enjoyed his bachelor life, the solitude was a strength for him. He hated people around all of the time, except for his mother. Now, she was in his head and offering her opinions about everything. On top of that he was worried about her, he didn't like that feeling, that connection it could only be dangerous. This whole thing was supposed to be about sex, even that went beyond what could be labeled as normal. She was both giver and taker and it had been the best experience of his life to date. He had a lot to think about and she made up most of it. He decided to do a little digging and find out more about her. It was probably crossing a line, but it would give him some piece of mind.

Monday came and the two of them went to work with very different missions in mind. She was determined to put the whole thing behind her and work hard. She was able to pay rent this month and could continue on that way, but if she moved to her parents house for a few months she could find something nicer, better, and less scary. She needed this to work, she had no other choices. She spent Sunday moving boxes into storage near her parents' house and all that was left were a few things she would need to survive for the next couple of weeks. She made her way to her desk and started logging into various sites. It was Linda's idea to start the day off that way. She glanced at his door, but made no move to bother him.

Byron was angry, and insulted. She used him. He could argue that he had used her too, but somewhere down deep he felt like he really connected to her. He made his way into the office passing her desk without saying a word. It would be hard to exist like this, her working for him. But if he fired her, she could stir up one hell of a lawsuit. He ran his hands through his hair, she was more than broke. She was in debt up to her ears and he even found where she tried to take out a number of loans but been denied. The final straw was finding an email where she detailed finding a solution to her problem, it was a note to herself really, but she had been looking for a solution. He would be damned if it would be him. He rubbed his eyes. He could feel a headache coming on, he would have to face her sooner or later. He buzzed her in. She came in professionally and sat across from him waiting for him to say something. He didn't even look up at her for the longest time. Finally, he did. She looked different somehow, she wore contacts today and let her silky hair flow down her shoulders just aching him to touch it. He shook his head.

"Miss Greene, there are some new events on the horizon for the company and there is a good chance you will be moving to a different department. I wanted to be the first to tell you, so that there was no confusion." He watched her eyes shooting at him like daggers as she crossed her arms over her chest.

"Really now, how convenient." She was angry and hurt, but mostly hurt. He used her and was now casting her off to a different department.

"It's completely out of my hands." He gave her a hard look.

"I bet it is. I can't believe I trusted you." She stood up and stomped her way back into her office.

She slammed the door shut behind her. It was just as well. Then she wouldn't have to deal with him all day, which would suit her just fine.

Still, it hurt. Her plan to seduce him and make her life easier had been more like something she told herself to make being with him easier. She never stood a chance of telling him no. She was really to blame for the whole situation. She went in that room, she stayed the night... she opened up to him. She looked around the desk. This would never work, not really. She put her head in her hands just as she heard him storm in.

"I can't believe you would say anything to me about trust, Miss Greene." His eyes were staring down at her hard.

"What are you talking about Blakemore, I was there... you led me to that room." She felt the tears welling up but she refused to let them fall.

"Oh no sweetheart, I take responsibility for that one. I'm talking about your plan, to "snare a good man" to help you with all of your problems. You're in debt up to your eyeballs." He was seething and she stood to defend herself.

"SO what, who cares if I am in debt, why is that your problem and how is it any of your business. Oh wait... you can't believe you had sex with someone who's not rich like you, is that it?" She felt as though someone kicked her in the stomach, she was humiliated.

He grabbed her arm and pulled her to him. "I don't care if I found you penniless on the street in rags, I would have still seen you, still made love to you" he let her go "still wanted you." He sighed running a hand through his hair. "My issue is not that you're poor Rachel, it's that you set a goal in mind. O,ne to catch me, and make me fix all your problems."

She stared at him a moment before the realization of what he'd done became apparent.

"What did you do Blakemore?" her eyes were on fire as she looked him over. "Did you do research on me or something? What was it a background check.... Credit check? I'm sure the list goes on and on doesn't it." She waited. "Not going to admit to it, I guess, what makes you think I wanted or needed you to rescue me, Mr. Blakemore?" She stood with her arms crossed over her chest.

He had the decency to look guilty before he told her. "I read your emails, I needed to know more about you."

She blushed, humiliated.

"You tell me the truth now Rachel, was that your plan all along? Suck me in and use me to feel safe, to be secure?"

She took a deep breath before she answered. "I wrote that as a note to myself, yes at first when you said those things to me the first day I was here, I did. I thought I'd beat you at your own game." She faced the window as she spoke, letting the tears fall now. "I thought, somehow I would show you I can be just like you. But I didn't, the minute I was in that room with you I lost the game. We both knew it and I accepted it. I cared about you, you can't just use someone you care about, it doesn't work that way." She wiped at her face and spun back around to face him. "But it is clear that you play dirty too, researching me like I'm one of your corporate mergers or something. Like I'm not real, and here, you don't trust anyone or anything and one day it will leave you cold and alone." She grabbed her purse and jacket. "Obviously this won't work, I'm sorry if you felt used... but then that's exactly how I feel too." She left quickly making her way to the elevator and then to her car.

She sat in the garage for a moment, letting it all sink in. Just a few short hours ago, she had been on cloud nine, developed something real. She was going to take back her life, she had new feelings for someone and job security. Now, it was all gone, all at once. At least it was early, she could go home and be depressed alone. She made her way to the apartment amazed at the transformation. The days were so peaceful, the nights were right out of a horror novel. She fell into her bed and finally let go. Her body wracked with sobs as she cried out her pain, her loss and for Blakemore.

Byron tried to work, he focused his thoughts solely on the project at hand, yet he realized he reread started the same page about 6 times. He pushed the papers away from him and sighed. The entire situation with Rachel was a mess. He knew she was sincere, she had started out with a plan, but once they were in that room, she let it go and chose him in that moment. He regretted it now, demanding an explanation and hurting her. She had been crying by the window, he wanted to pull her close, but he couldn't move. Nothing in his life had been like this and he wasn't sure how to act. On top of all that he was out an assistant, again. He called down to HR and asked Alice to come up. He was still lost in thought when she opened the door. She sashayed into the room and made her way over to him, running her hands down his chest. He suddenly realized what she was doing and stopped her hands.

"Not today Alice, I need a new assistant. Can you start making some calls please?" He looked up at her and they knew it was done. Looking at her now he felt nothing, no excitement.

"So the little bookworm fled the scene did she? Fine, I'll hire you a new assistant." She started to leave.

"Alice." She stopped but didn't turn around. "This between us... its done." She turned and gave him a smile.

"I knew that the minute you hired her yourself Byron, I just had to try." She left the room.

He frowned. It seemed as though everyone knew him better that he knew himself. He had work to do, but he couldn't think straight. Fortunately, he had a few meetings at least that would take his mind off of her. She was right, it was better this way. They couldn't work together, not when every time he saw her he wanted to touch her. He glanced up at the clock and made his way to the conference hall.

The day went by slowly, Rachel felt every minute of it. She was hungry and yet she didn't want to move. She was always the strong one, always rolled with the punches, but something about Byron Blakemore left her shattered. She knew she was going to move, she'd lost her job and by the weekend she would be on her mother's couch amid the hugs and "I'm sorry's" she would likely receive from them all. Just that alone was enough, but admitting she was in love with Blakemore was the culprit of her current state. He was an ass, he was also kind and sweet and horribly romantic. She knew there was a connection from day one and instead of walking away from it... she dove in with both feet... right into a golden love nest practically on top of the world. She knew that at the very least, she would have that night, with him. She must have fallen asleep finally, because the next thing she knew there was a huge noise coming from down the hall. She jumped out of bed and hearing the yelling she made her way to the door. She heard men fighting, loudly and she immediately braced the door with a chair and hid in her closet. She dialed 911 and waited.

Byron was exhausted. He made his way into his lavish house and found his mother sitting in the living room watching television. If there was anyone who knew him, really knew, him it was her. She glanced up at him and he gave her a smile. His entire life she had been a constant for him. Always there no matter what. When he was little she always managed to scrape it together so that they had food and a place to sleep.

Sometimes nicer places than others. He would always take care of her no matter what.

"Momma, how was your day? Did the new lady come?" He slumped down beside her.

"Oh yes, she was delightful she brought some cards and I beat her every time." She glanced at him and chuckled loudly.

"Good Mom, I'm glad, I feel better knowing someone is around while I'm not." He sighed and she turned the volume down on the television.

"Ok son spill it, what's wrong?" He looked over at her and shook his head. "You can try and tell me nothing but it will just put off this conversation longer. Talk to me boy." She gave him a nudge with her elbow and he smiled at her.

"It's about a woman." He saw her sit up quickly.

"A woman, well, I'd say it's about time then." She gave him a pat. "Go on what's wrong."

"I met her and then hired her, things got... involved." He gave her a look and she rolled her eyes.

"It always does. Keep going."

"Well, she had a plan, initially, to somehow make me fall for her or something and then get her out of her problems. So I called her out on it after I found out."

"How did you find this out son?" She looked at him thoughtfully.

He blushed. "I did a bunch of background checks and emails and stuff." He looked away.

"I see. Go on."

"Well, I confronted her and she got upset and quit and told me she was trying to get me back to playing games with her." He looked over at her, she was smiling.

"I like this girl already." She laughed lightly. "I'm sorry son, you can hardly be mad at someone for getting you back. Were you playing a game?"

"I don't think so, I mean I just like things a certain way. I don't want to get too involved, I've seen how relationships can be."

She took a deep breath before she answered. "Byron your daddy was a silly man who didn't care about anyone. He took what he wanted and left the world behind, including you and me." He nudged him again to get his attention. "Love wasn't the problem, or relationships honey, it was being afraid of them that drove him away and made him run like the devil. What you're trying to avoid, feeling something, loving someone... that was what made him the way he was." She took his face in her hands." I am getting old Byron baby, I need me some grandkids before I'm gone, don't stop your heart from feeling or you will be just like the man you detest." She let him go.

He sat thinking, then he noticed the flashes on the television. He only watched for a second before he felt his heart stop and his body go cold. That was Rachel's apartment building.

"Mom turn it up." She saw him freeze and she did so quickly.

They watched together, the news was covering a shooting that had happened in the building leaving some of the tenants either dead or injured. The entire building was considered a crime scene upon discovering a meth lab in the basement as the police raided and finally caught the shooter.

"Son, what is it?" She touched his arm concerned.

"That's her building, that's where Rachel lives. I have to go mom, I'll be back, I love you." He grabbed his coat and ran from the penthouse.

He knew he was speeding as he made his way to her building. The police were still there and people were everywhere. He combed the area looking for her hoping to see her. He needed to tell her, needed to protect her. He should have never let go in there in the first place. The day after their overnight at the hotel he should have stormed in there and pulled her back out with him. He was frantic as he raked his hand through his hair. If anything happened to her...

"Blakemore, what the hell are you doing here?" He spun around at the voice and she stood there draped in a blanket.

He didn't say a word he simply grabbed her and pulled her to him. He looked her over checking for signs that she was hurt. He kissed her then not giving her a chance to speak or move. It was a quick and hard kiss, something to prove that she was real, and she was ok.

"You're not hurt." It was more of a statement than anything.

"No, I'm fine, what are you doing here?" She stood there waiting for an answer he heart beating erratically from the kiss.

"I saw the news, I was worried about you. I came as soon as I found out. You're sure you're ok?" He held her head in his hands.

"I said I'm fine, Byron. Why did you come? You think I'm awful, yet you're here, and kissing me?"

"I love you." He said it simply.

"You what? Don't be ridiculous, Byron. Just this morning you were ready to kill me." She turned to go but he grabbed her arm.

"I am an idiot Rachel, I was so angry, because, I am in love with you. When I thought you didn't feel anything for me and I was just a means to an end it hurt, and I equated that to anger."

She was crying, he said he loved her but did he mean it? She looked at him in his designer suit, ruined with dirt and she'd never seen him look so disheveled. She looked at his eyes as he gazed down on her full of love.

"I love you too, Byron." She gave him a half smile. He scooped her up and spun her around.

"First things first, you are not living here anymore." He said it very matter-of-factly.

She felt her temper rise, he was already bossing her around. They started walking towards his car.

"Wait, how did you even know I lived here?" He kept walking.

"I followed you the day after the hotel." She stopped.

"You what!" He pulled her along to the car.

"I know I'm horrible, let's just go home." Before she could protest about his snooping, she felt the warmth of his lips on hers and she knew that home was exactly where she was.

The Billionaire's Gift

April's mind still reeled from the news. It was all anyone in her sorority house talked about, and all that she saw on the news. Lewis Edwards had been arrested and charged with securities fraud. It turned out that the investment scheme he was running truly was a scheme – a Ponzi scheme. He was bringing in new investors, most of them hardworking middle class looking to build retirement funds, and using the money to pay his high net worth investors. It all came crashing down on him, and in an attempt to pay back as much of the money as they could, the Feds seized all of Edwards' assets.

The problem for April was that Lewis Edwards was her father.

April would never have considered herself rich, but she was wealthy. They had enough money that she never worried about anything. She never even questioned why her mother left her father five years ago – though she suspected now that her mother got wise to his scheme and decided to leave. April felt badly now for insisting to stay with him. She had alienated her mother, and right now, she could have used a sympathetic shoulder to cry on.

Everyone had abandoned her. Her boyfriend of two years broke up with her which led to a hefty weight gain. Her friends turned their backs on her. April was alone and miserable. As the spring semester wrapped up, April somehow managed to make it through her finals and wondered what would happen next. Would she be able to come back to school? Would she even have a place to live? The home she had known her whole life was locked up and taped. It and everything inside was to be auctioned off this summer.

April sat on the bed of her dorm room and looked out the window. Her roommate Sylvia had already left. Sylvia had hardly said a word to her since the news about her father came out. Of all of her friends, April thought Sylvia had the best reason. Her father had been one of the investors in the Edwards Fund, and he very likely lost a great deal of money.

The day outside was bright, far brighter than April felt. She let out a long sigh. She had held off on calling her mother. She knew that her mother would not turn her away, but she was also not sure how she was going to get to her. She was across the country now, in California. While she had managed to pick up her life, April doubted that she would be able to spring for a plane ticket at the last minute.

"You're still here," a light voice said from April's doorway.

April turned to see her sorority sister Chloe standing there. She was holding a suitcase in one hand and a box under her other arm.

"Yeah, I'm not in any hurry to get nowhere," April said.

Chloe set her things down at the doorway and walked over to Sylvia's old bed. She sat down and looked at April, measuring her carefully. April was not sure what to make of it. She and Chloe were never close. Chloe was a year her senior and a sweet girl, but the two of them had almost nothing in common.

"It's been hard on you the last few weeks," Chloe said at last. "Do you know where you're going?"

April shrugged her shoulders. "I'll probably call my mom out in California and see if I can join her out there."

Chloe frowned. "That's a long way to go for an 'if you can.'"

April appreciated Chloe's ability to quickly understand a situation; even she did not understand all of the details behind it. It did not help her though, and April let out another deep sigh before looking out the window again.

"You know," Chloe said, "I might have a solution for you."

April turned back to face Chloe. A solution was just what she needed. "What's that?"

"My dad owns a resort upstate. He always needs extra help for the summer, and it pays really well. You also get to stay at the resort free, though you're staying in the servants quarters. It's not too bad, as long as you don't mind spending your summer in a room about the size of this dorm room."

April never had to work a summer job. She was aware of the concept, but the practice itself was alien to her. Still, the idea of getting a job had a certain appeal. It meant that she did not have to depend on her mother, and if her mother saw her trying to make an effort to get past everything and be better for it, it might help the two of them repair their relationship. If her mother could help, she might even be willing to do it on more even terms than April having to move somewhere strange.

"Will it be a problem, to get me a job I mean?" April asked.

Chloe shook her head. "My dad's opinion is that anyone who can't ask a few simple questions about an investment probably deserves to lose their money." Chloe paused and gave April an apologetic look. "It's a harsh opinion. But it means that he's not going to have anything against helping you. Besides, nothing that happened had anything to do with you. It was all your father."

April gave Chloe the first real smile that she felt in weeks. "Thank you so much. Whatever he needs me to do, I don't care. I'll even wash toilets."

Chloe laughed. "It won't be that bad. It'll be hard work, but the resort is beautiful, and staff always get two days off during the week, so you'll even get to enjoy some of it."

April did not care about getting to enjoy the resort. For the first time since the investigation into her father started, April was starting to see the light at the end of a very dark tunnel.

She even thought it might not be a train.

****

April had never had the opportunity to visit Stuart Estates before. It was far more upscale than anything her family would have afforded, though she knew many of her father's clients probably frequented this resort. She wished she had gotten to see and enjoy it without having to be an employee. Set in a mountain valley, it featured a large manor house that hosted any number of events, from conferences to weddings and family reunions. Some of the upstairs rooms were still held as private rooms for guests, though a majority of guest accommodations were in "cabins," buildings that had once served as guest houses or were built later when the original property was converted.

Still, April thought that she would enjoy working here. The air was crisp and clear. She was surrounded by beauty. It was tranquil, even if her supervisor Henry Graven did promise that she would be far too busy to take notice of what was around them.

Mr. Graven was a cold man, tall with pale skin and dark hair. April recognized the name right away, and did her best not to cringe. He was one of the people who lost their retirement money to her father's scheme. She could tell by the way that he looked at her; he knew who she was. He would not be able to do anything overt, but if she gave him any reason to fire her, he would not hesitate to take it.

Her first day was mostly a learning curve, of going from being the person waited on to doing the waiting. Mr. Graven was grudgingly patient as she learned, and she found the rest of the staff to be kind and understanding. She did not think any of them knew about her circumstances, and she was thankful for that. It was still a stressful day, and she was happy to retire in the evening to her room.

Her "room" was one-half of a small cabin that April thought had probably been a campground cabin at some point. Now it was fitted with lighting and a small window unit to control heat and air. A bathroom had also been built onto it, to be shared between the two units. It was small, smaller than her dorm room had been, but it was comfortable, brightly decorated, and most of all private.

April lay on her bed and thought about her day. It has been busy. Mr. Graven was right. She had barely had time to notice the beautiful scenery around her. She decided she would change that. She would give herself a few days to get used to the job, and after that, she would take brief moments in her day to just appreciate where she was.

****

April knelt down to wipe up the spilled coffee and gather up the shards of china cups that were now scattered about the floor. She was still getting used to carrying trays and keeping them balanced. Something had brushed her thigh over her skirt – it was not a something, it was a man's hand, she was certain of that – and caused her to lose her balance. Now, she was mortified as guests watched her fumbling with the glass shards and spilt coffee, trying hard not to cut herself.

When the last piece was gathered and the last of the coffee sopped up, April stood, careful not to tip her tray and spill any of the shards. As she walked past a table, she felt a hand brush the top of her knee. She glanced back to see an older man with short, thick grey hair give her a wink. She quickly turned, trying to control her blush and pushed through the swinging doors back into the kitchen galley.

"Are you okay?" Leah, one of the other girls on staff asked her as she set down her tray of broken cups.

"A guest is getting grabby," April said. She let out a sigh as she began to move the shards into the collection bin set up for broken wares. "It just caught me off guard, that's all."

"You should be more careful with your tray Miss Edwards." Mr. Graven paused as he walked past her. "You are lucky that you did not burn anyone."

"I'm sorry. I'll be more careful next time," April said.

She did not look up to see Mr. Graven's look, but she was sure it was one of contempt. He walked on and she finished depositing the shards and took her tray to be washed. Another tray of coffee was set up, which Leah picked up to take out. April was relieved. She did not want to have to go back out into the dining room right now, not right on the heels of something so embarrassing.

The rest of the noon day brunch went by smoothly, and when April did have to go back out, she was glad to see that guests paid her no more attention than they did to any other member of staff. Slowly the guests filed out of the dining hall and out to the veranda. It was still raining lightly outside, but it would clear soon. The guests would enjoy any number of outdoor festivities while the staff prepared the indoor rooms for evening festivities.

April moved to her area of the dining room and began cleaning the tables. Someone else would come behind to vacuum, but she wanted to make sure that the floor was cleared of any large debris. As with everything else, she was still getting accustomed to cleaning, and the rest of the staff were done and cleared away as she still worked, her mind turning over bits of half-remembered lyrics to keep her moving at a steady pace.

A hand moved over the small of April's back and along her buttock. She jumped up, pushing into the bulk of someone behind her. April had not even heard anyone come up on her. When she turned, she saw the same man with the grabby hands from brunch.

"You're like a little rabbit." His voice was smooth as he spoke. His eyes were even and demanding. April gripped the table and tried to put space between them, only to have him close it again. "I do like hunting rabbits."

"I need to finish my work." April could not think of anything else to say. The man's hands moved to her waist and slowly up her sides to cup her breasts.

Everything happened at once then. The swinging door from the kitchen galley opened. Mr. Graven walked out, followed by two other staff members. The door from the veranda opened and an older woman walked in, followed by two young men. April's hand collided with the face of the man accosting her with a loud slap propelled by the swing of her arm. It resounded through the dining hall before the woman began to scream shrilly.

April tried to wrestle control of her situation, but she could not. Mr. Graven was upon the scene immediately, asking the man – Henry Worthington as it turned out to April's surprise and horror – if he were okay. The woman screamed about a trollop hitting her husband. Mr. Worthington began his explanation of how she had come onto him. April tried to speak up, to give her side of the story, only to be hushed by Mr. Graven or Mrs. Worthington screaming about lies. The noise brought more guests from the veranda into the dining room.

Mr. Graven finally took hold of April's arm, squeezing tightly and leading her away. She tried to protest over his assurances to Mr. Worthington that he would take care of the situation. He led her out into the hall and spun her around hard, slamming her back against the wall and knocking the air from her. Further down, guests poured out of the dining room and into the hall, not wanting to miss the end of the drama.

"I have been very patient with you, but I will not have you accosting our guests," Mr. Graven kept his voice stern and even.

"I didn't do anything wrong," April said.

"You slapped one of the resorts most honored guests. You will go up to him and you will apologize."

"I will not. The man is a pig!" April said louder than she meant to.

Mr. Graven pulled back his hand and aware of the crowd stopped himself. He lowered his voice and leaned in closer to April. "You are fired, do you understand? You will go to your cabin and pack your belongings. I expect to see you gone from here within the hour."

April could not say anything else. She turned and ran down the hall as tears began to stream from her eyes, burning her cheeks in her shame and embarrassment.

****

Nigel Conroy knew two things very well. Henry Worthington was a misogynist and a womanizer and the staff of Stuart would happily kiss the ground that he walked on. He was certain that Worthington could have murdered the poor girl and the staff supervisor would still have found a way to claim she had fallen upon his knife or gun herself.

He also had a very good idea of who the girl was. He face was familiar, one he knew he had seen recently on the news. If he was right, she had been through enough. Being fired in front of all of the guests here was the last thing she needed. As the crowd began to slowly disperse, he took hold of the arm of another staff, a cute young woman with short blonde hair.

"I'm sorry, but I wanted to ask you something before you had a chance to go away," Nigel said, releasing her.

"It's alright sir," the young woman said. "How can I help you?"

"The girl that just ran down the hall, what was her name?"

The young woman narrowed her eyes, and Nigel did not blame her. He sensed protectiveness and found himself very much liking this young woman.

"I don't mean any harm, but she didn't deserve what happened, and I think you know it. I'm pretty sure I've seen you here for a few seasons, so I think you know what really happened. I just want to make sure she'll be okay."

The young woman continued to eye him warily. Nigel did his best to project his sincerity and she finally relaxed. "April Edwards. I can take you to see her. We share the same cabin."

Nigel nodded his head. "Thank you. If anyone says anything, just tell them I pulled you aside to help me with an errand. I'll vouch for you, I promise."

The young woman did not say anything else. She simply turned and Nigel understood he was expected to follow her. She led him through a side door of the main estate house. The morning rain was now stopped, and the humidity of the afternoon was quickly setting in. She kept a brisk pace as she led him to the servant's cabins and to what he presumed to be her own.

Nigel stepped in to a small living area with a couch, chair, and television and three doors that along the two adjacent and one opposite walls.

The young woman turned to the left door and knocked gently. "April sweetie, it's Leah."

"Please go away, Leah. I don't want to talk to anyone," April's muffled voice came through the door, thick with her tears.

Leah looked back at Nigel but he nodded, waving his hand to urge her to continue.

"April, there's a man here to see you," Leah said.

The door swung open and April appeared, her face streaked with tears and fire in her eyes. Nigel felt a great deal of respect for her suddenly, and felt very badly for anyone that earned that ire. He thought she could have a fiery temper, one she might not even be aware of.

"I'll gouge out that bastard's eyes if it's him," April said before her eyes had a chance to survey the room. When they fell on Nigel, some of the fire pulled back, though he noticed it did not withdraw completely. "Who is that?"

"He's one of the guests," Leah said. "He wanted to make sure you were okay."

April stood there and studied Nigel before turning back to her friend. "Tell him I'll be fine."

"Can I speak to you for a few minutes?" Nigel took a step forward.

Leah looked from Nigel to April, and he could see the helplessness in her eyes. She had duties to attend to and could not be playing referee between them.

April sighed and placed a hand on Leah's shoulder. "It's fine. You get back up before you get into trouble too."

Leah hesitated, looked between the two of them again. She finally nodded. "You find me before you go, okay?"

"I will. Thank you." April gave Leah a hug. She released her and Leah walked past Nigel, giving him a careful look that he read very well. April had a bad enough day, and he did not need to make it worse.

As Leah walked out of the cabin, Nigel turned his attention to the young woman before him as she stepped out of her room. She wore only the simple black dress common to all of the staff. The white apron had been discarded somewhere, either in her room or thrown aside as she fled the shameful scene.

"You have a good friend. Have the two of you known each other a long time?" Nigel was curious about this young woman. The media had painted her as the aloof princess of a sinister financial king, carefully keeping herself out of the direct light of the media. He was not seeing that here. He was seeing something vastly different.

"Just a few days. Leah is a real gem, though." April tilted her head to one side. "What are you doing here?"

Nigel gave a small laugh. "You're not going to ask who I am?"

April shook her head. "I know who you are. Your face shows up in almost every magazine, usually some story about a broken-hearted girl or a large playboy party."

Nigel brought his hand up to his chest and feigned injury. "You wound me. But that's fair enough. I won't lie. I know who you are too."

April frowned deeply. "Here to gloat then?"

A sharp pain stabbed through Nigel's chest and he was surprised to feel it. He was not sure why he felt so much sympathy for this young woman. She was attractive. Her dark hair and bright, blue eyes would be enough to captivate any man. Something else had drawn him in, however. He just wished that he could put his finger on what it was.

"No," Nigel said simply. "I really did want to make sure you were okay. Do you know what you're going to do?"

April shook her head. "I can't go back down to New York. My face is still all over the television. I guess I get to hope that the few days of pay I have here is enough to fly me out to Los Angeles."

"You don't have anyone that can help you out?" Nigel felt very badly for her now. He knew from the news reports that her father's assets had all been seized. He never imagined that it would leave her destitute. He wondered if anyone had bothered to care about that.

"I talked to my mother. She's working as a waitress and trying to get into acting. She barely has enough money to pay her bills." April paused. "Why am I tell you this?"

Why am I about to do what I'm about to do? Nigel was glad to see that at least both of them were behaving in ways they did not understand. She had an excuse. She was under duress. He had no idea what his excuse was, but he knew he would not be able to stop himself now.

"Would you like to spend the rest of the week here with me, as my guest?" Nigel asked.

April's look of shock made him smile. "What?"

Nigel took in a deep breath and let it out. "I'm not sure why your supervisor was so hard on you, but I'm sure that you did not have it coming. A few broken cups is not worth risking a sexual harassment lawsuit. You don't have anywhere else to go right now. So, take a few days to figure it out. Maybe you and your mother will be able to work out something. In the meantime, enjoy the resort as a guest where your old boss can't touch you. As for Mr. Worthington, have the best revenge you can have on him."

April crossed her arms. "What's that?"

"Show him that it had no ill effect on you. Show him that you're over it and moved on. People who do things like that; they thrive on knowing the chaos they've caused."

Nigel watched April carefully as she considered his proposal. She was wary, and he did not blame her. He knew how quickly people in his own circles could turn if the sensed weakness or unattractive controversy. He did not expect that people in hers would be any different.

She finally uncrossed her arms and gave him a square look, setting her shoulders even. "What's the catch?"

Nigel shook his head. "No catch. You'll have to stay with me, but I have one of the luxury cabins, so you'll have your own room. No expectations, except that you'll accompany me and keep me company. That's all."

April continued to study him carefully. Finally, her stance relaxed. "Okay. I'll accept your invitation."

Nigel nodded. "Good. Do you have street clothes?"

April laughed. "Nothing worthy of a place like this."

"Then I'll add one more caveat to this deal. Allow me to take you into town for a shopping trip."

April nodded. Nigel sat down to wait for her to gather her things. This was a quaint and small cabin. He wondered if she had a chance to see the luxury guest cabins yet, and what she would make of them.

****

April held her shopping bags in her hand as she followed Nigel up the walkway to the large cabin. Large picture windows dominated the façade, glowing through their translucent white shades. He carried her suitcase and occasionally made as though to be bearing too heavy of a weight. She could only laugh at that.

Nigel Conroy the man was nothing like the man in so many magazine articles that she and her sorority sisters would read. She thought he could have his arrogant side, and occasionally as he took her through the shops in town, she saw it, typically, when he put down a dress or outfit because he felt the price tag was too low. Mostly, he was normal, if somewhat impulsive in taking her on as his guest.

He opened the door to the cabin and held it for her to walk in.

It opened immediately to the main room, open with a vaulted ceiling. A large fireplace dominated it with a couch and two oversized chairs set in front of it. A wide high definition television hung above the fireplace and a full entertainment system sat to the left side. Along the left wall stood a bar and to her right the room opened to a dining room and a kitchen. April wondered if it saw use at all and wondered at its inclusion.

A stairway led up in front of her, dividing the mysterious kitchen from the rest of the downstairs. Nigel closed the door behind them and led her up the stairs. To her right another large living area was set up with balcony rails do that it looked down below them. Beyond it was a hall with three doors. Nigel guided her to one and invited her to set down her things. A double bed sat in this room and a elegant dresser. She set her bags down beside the door as Nigel set her suitcase down by the dresser.

"There's a bathroom right across the hall from you. If you don't like this bed, you can try the one in the room next to you. My room is at the end of the hall. I don't know if you do your own laundry. If you do, the French doors in the hall have a small washer and dryer behind them. You can also set your laundry in the bins outside for staff to pick up. It's your choice, but I do my own laundry."

April blinked her eyes. "You do your own laundry?" She tried to imagine this man measuring out detergent and could not imagine it.

"My housekeeper at home taught me after I ruined my own clothes at another resort. I've had bad luck with staff losing my things."

April wondered if his items were lost or taken. Most of the staff here were honest and hardworking, but she supposed that anyone could be tempted to take something that belonged to someone famous. "I suppose you cook too."

Nigel shook his head. "No, that's never a pretty sight. I hoped you did, actually."

April laughed and shook her head. "My cooking is part of our sorority's hazing ritual." She watched as he gave her a dubious look, tilting his head to one side. "I'm serious. I once boiled the coating out of a pan."

Nigel leaned against the doorframe, his look becoming quickly serious and contemplative. "It's not fair, you know."

"I know. I have to be more careful with pots." April wanted the levity. The look in his eyes unsettled her.

"I'm serious. It's fine that the Feds want to make sure your father pays back the money that he's taken. That's good. They can't take away his ability to care for the people he's responsible for. That punishes you for something you didn't do."

April swallowed hard. She did not like the look in Nigel's eyes right now. It made her want to probe and want to understand the depth of empathy that he had in this moment. She did not want to do that. He was being nice to do this for her, but she did not want to complicate things any more than they were already complicated for her.

"Right," Nigel pushed himself from the doorframe. "You've had a busy day, so I'll let you rest. I'll wake you up in the morning and we can go and enjoy brunch and some horseback riding if you like."

"Horseback riding would be nice," April said. "Thank you again."

Nigel smiled as he turned to the hall. "Thank you for accepting my invitation."

****

The young boy stood in front of the blazing fire, his eyes picking up the orange flames, reflecting them back to the world. Tears streamed down his soot-covered face and when he coughed, he sounded congested and full of smoke. Inside, in the flames, was everything he ever knew and understood to be love, compassion, and order. He could not understand what was happening, or why Nana uttered apologies as she tried to clean the soot from his face.

April sat up in bed and took in a deep breath. Vivid dreams did not come on often, but when they did, they always left her feeling strange, as though she were coming back into her own body. It was, she thought, the effect of her mind moving from its dream reality back into the real world.

The dream bothered her, and as her day played back in her mind and she remembered where she was, she understood why.

She had found the story by chance. Her ex-boyfriend had a playboy magazine sitting on his bed, and she flipped through to the life story of Nigel Conroy, as promised on the cover, while he played on his game console. When Nigel was five years old, his mother had set fire to their home. She had drugged her husband and her son's nanny. She spread kerosene through the house, then over herself and her husband, lighting the both of them on fire. As the fire spread, Nigel's cries somehow managed to wake the groggy nanny, who stumbled out of the inferno, holding the crying child.

The image in her dream was an image from the magazine article, a picture that had been taken of the boy as he stood watching the inferno that had been his home. He said in the interview for the article that he did not really remember the day, but it still influenced his life. His mother suffered from mental illness, untreated because both her family and his father had considered the idea of mental illness to be shameful, something that others faced, not them. Nigel had inherited his father's fortune, and when he was old enough to decide a direction for it, created a foundation to encourage the treatment and de-stigmatization of mental illness.

How could she have forgotten such a terrible, tragic story? April put her head in her hands and began crying.

****

April followed Nigel up to the main estate house, where brunch waited for them. She wondered what Mr. Graven would make of her being there, or Leah for that matter. She thought about Chloe, who had gotten her the job to begin with. She hoped that Chloe was not told about what had happened. She hated to think that she would be made to regret helping her.

Brunch was a pleasant affair, full of conversation. They sat at a large table with other resort guests and engaged in polite conversation. A few of the people at her table knew who April was, but none of them seemed to think her situation warranted more than a passing acknowledgement. She was happy for that. She noticed a glare from Mr. Graven. When he attempted to come to the table, Nigel rose and pulled him aside quickly. April did not know what was said exactly, only that it began with, "before you embarrass yourself."

After brunch, they followed the other guests out to the veranda. There was no rain today, and the early afternoon was quickly growing warm. April followed Nigel through the crowd of people as he walked the direction of the stables.

Mr. Worthington backed up, separating her from Nigel and almost causing April to run into him. He turned, startled, and gave her a kindly smile. "My apologies miss. My son was just clowning around as boys are want to do."

"That's okay, Mr. Worthington," April said carefully.

Mr. Worthington blinked his eyes and gave April a broader smile. "Well, I'm afraid you have me at a loss. You know me, but I don't know you."

April smiled, feeling strange and light. After the huge scene the day before, he did not even recognize her face. She supposed that in the world Mr. Worthington inhabited, it was impossible that a woman who was a servant the day before could be a guest today.

She supposed he had never seen Cinderella.

"I'm afraid I'll have to leave it that way," April said. She glided past Mr. Worthington before he could stay anything else. Nigel had stopped and turned. He was now waiting on her, his look quickly becoming confused as she walked up to him.

"What happened?" he asked.

"I just bumped into Mr. Worthington," April said and decided to laugh. "He didn't even recognize me."

Nigel blinked his eyes and tilted his head. April continued on to the steps that led down from the veranda. The stables were ahead, and she wanted to smell the fresh hay and the horses. Mr. Worthington did not think enough of the day to even realize she and the servant he tried to molest were the same person.

If he could not be bothered, she supposed she did not need to either. The thought of putting the incident behind her lightened her step. After weeks of being remembered, a single moment of being forgotten was bliss.

****

Nigel's horse bucked and he pulled up on the reigns to gain control again, watching the young woman who laughed, carefree on the back of her own. She pulled up on the reigns and turned her horse so that she could twist in her saddle to look at him. This time yesterday, she was in tears. Now, she could have been a completely different person. Nigel supposed in a way, she was. All she needed was a glass slipper and they could have been a prince and princess in a fairy tale.

"You shouldn't look so serious," April said. "Horseback riding is supposed to be fun."

"There's fun, and then there's slapping my horse's rump and startling him," Nigel said, but he found her smile to be infectious.

April shrugged her shoulders. "You were riding like an old man. I just wanted to see if you really knew how to ride."

Nigel took in a breath and nodded his head, recognizing the challenge. "I know how to ride, my dear. I took my first lesson at ten years old."

"Seven," April gave him a smug look.

"I still have you on years riding," Nigel said. He was only about six years older than April was, but his pride was wounded now.

They continued their ride along the forest trail and up the mountain. It was beautiful here, and being out here among the natural beauty seemed to have a good effect on April. Nigel was not sure that he understood why her encounter with Mr. Worthington had left her in such a good mood, but it was nice to see that the forest around them was keeping it in place.

They reached the water trough for the horses and dismounted, tying their reigns off on the poles there so the horses could drink and relax. This stop in the ride was along the ridge of the mountain that the horse trail wound. It offered a nice view of the valley and the estate below, and Nigel was happy to see that few others were taking advantage of the stables today. Most were heading out to the cricket grounds or down to the lake.

Nigel turned to look at April, and saw that she was watching him. The look in her eyes was deep and sympathetic. He wondered at it, but was not sure what to ask her. Perhaps she was feeling badly about spooking his horse.

"This is really nice," April said. She turned and looked back over the valley below them. "I really do appreciate you doing this for me."

Nigel stepped up to her and took her hand in his. She did not pull away, and he held it tighter. As they looked over the valley, she talked about horseback riding in the boroughs outside of New York City and spending her entire weekend learning how to care for the horses. It was, she admitted to him, the only chore she ever learned to do, and one that she always loved.

With her face in profile to him, Nigel could see that she was deeper in her thoughts than her words expressed. Was she remembering the good times with her father and mother, or was it just her father? He realized he had no idea how long her mother had been in Los Angeles. It could have been weeks or years. He had the feeling from how she had talked about her prospects of getting there that they two of them were not very close.

April turned to face him, and Nigel found himself caught by her eyes. They were deep and contemplative while bright, catching the sky above them. Nigel brought his hand up to her face, cupping her cheek. He did not think about what he was doing. He simply leaned forward to kiss her.

****

Nigel's kiss was soft and careful, and it moved through April's body quickly, drawing her free hand up to his shoulders. Between her legs, she felt warm and alive. Nigel released her hand and moved his arm around her body, pressing her ample body closer to him. She could feel him hard against her and her own desire flared, surprising, and delighting her.

He broke away and looked down into her eyes. April wanted his kiss again, and with a flush realized that she wanted more. She imagined their bodies entwined together here along the mountain ridge, where other riders could come upon them at any moment. The idea tingling and warmth between her legs grow and she reached up to kiss him again, finding him responsive and welcoming.

Nigel brought his hand down from her face to her breast and cupped it gently. April wrapped her arms around his neck, running her fingers through Nigel's brown hair and lacing it through her fingers. He squeezed her breast and held her firm against him. April wanted him. She wanted to feel his hands caress her body, to feel him deep inside her. Her body ached and screamed its want, and as the pounding of hooves came up the mountain trail, she could not pull away from him.

They broke their kiss as another pair of riders came up to the trough. April flushed again and looked from Nigel to the newcomers.

"That must be some view," the woman said as she dismounted her horse. She tied it off next to Nigel's own and looked at her partner. "Do you think we can take a look over the ridge too?"

April stifled her laugh and took Nigel's hand, guiding him back to the horses. As they untied theirs from the trough, the new couple moved over to the ridge, sitting on the stone bench. April mounted her horse and waited for Nigel to join her. She considered heading back, but she wanted to push up the mountain. Yes, she wanted Nigel, and she thought if she told him she wanted to go back to his cabin now that he would. She also understood that part of that want came from moments like this, riding together and enjoying each other's company.

She could let it build.

They continued up the mountain trail, passing the new couple as the man put his arm around his companion. April supposed that the view really was romantic. She hoped there would be other such views on their way up.

They rode for another hour, and April could feel the heat of the day working into her body. A stream snaked along the slope of the mountain, coming close to the trail and skirting away from time to time. She thought about the hour, and how nice it would be to have a shower before they went up to the estate house for dinner. When she made the suggestion to Nigel that they head back, he was reluctant at first, until she mentioned showers. The look in his eye brought a new tingle between April's thighs.

As they made their way back down the mountain, they passed the couple that had come up to the water trough. They exchanged waves and continued on, stopping only briefly at the trough to allow the horses to get water. April's mind kept turning to the shower waiting for them, and she did not want to stop any longer than necessary. She thought of water on her skin and Nigel caressing her body and grew impatient to be back.

When they made it back down to the stables, the hands there took the horses from them, removing their tack and rubbing them down gently. They made their way across the estate grounds to the guest cabins, and April looked at Nigel. She could tell that he had something on his mind, and she wanted to be through it before they reached the cabin.

"Is something the matter?" April asked. She could not think of any other way to get conversation starting.

Nigel looked at her and gave her a gentle smile. "It was a beautiful ride, but I'm afraid I was a bit," he paused and looked up to find the words he needed, "presumptuous."

April took in a deep breath and nodded her head. Oh, to get him to see how much she wanted that kiss. She did not want to come across as someone easy, or who was trying to get something from him, but she knew exactly what she wanted from the rest of her evening.

"I told you I wasn't going to make any demands, and here I am crossing that line." Nigel placed his hands in his pockets. "It's not fair to you."

April twisted up her lips in thought and nodded again. "It's not." When he snapped his head to her, she gave him a smile. "Well, it wouldn't be if I weren't receptive to it."

Nigel narrowed his eyes and gave her a smile. He took her hand and picked up his pace. When they reached his cabin, he opened the door and she walked inside. When he closed the door behind them, his arms were around her body, pulling her back against him. April sighed and eased her stance so that she could feel his hardness pressing against her.

"I want you so badly I can taste it," Nigel whispered into her ear. He nibbled the lobe gently.

April turned around in his arms and brought her hands up to his shoulders. He pulled her tighter against him and April rose up to kiss him again. His tongue moved between her lips and danced with hers. She could taste his desire in his breath and wanted to drown in it. She brought her hands around to the collar of his shirt and slowly worked her way down his buttons.

When he broke the kiss, Nigel lifted April's shirt above her head, discarding it to the side and shedding his own. He moved his hands down to her waist and unbuttoned her shorts, pushing them down her body. He started to kneel, and a panic filled April.

"I'm sweaty from the ride," April said. She wanted what his kneeling offered, but she wanted it to be perfect.

Nigel stood. "Then let's have that shower."

He pushed down her shorts and underwear in one motion. April slipped out of her shoes and her clothing, releasing the catch of her bra behind her back and dropping that as well. She was naked before Nigel, and as his eyes took in her body, she shuddered, nervous. Would he find her extra weight pleasing, or would he be turned off by her curves?

"You are beautiful." Nigel placed his hands at her waist and pulled her to him again. He kissed her deeply and then released her, gesturing her to walk up the stairs. He guided her back to his bedroom with its oversized king bed dominating the room, and then to the bathroom beyond.

A large garden tub stood at one end of the bathroom. Next to it was a double size shower with stone tiling. April stepped up to it, and twisted the knobs on either side to start the water. Nigel stepped up behind her and she could feel him, naked now, pressing against her. She stepped into the shower and he followed.

Nigel took a large sponge and poured soap on it, lathering it in the stream of water that sprinkled over them. He brought it to April's body and caressed, leaving the soapy lather behind to be quickly washed away by the water. He moved along her chest, her arms, and her torso before moving down between and down her legs. When he finished, his lips were there, at her sex taking it in. April gasped and pressed her hands to the wall to support herself. His mouth was magic there, drawing her desire out of her and building it into a wave to crash over her body. She shivered as her body counted every bead of water that struck her.

When he stood, April took the sponge from him, lathering it again, and running it across his shoulders, down his torso, and up his back. She brought it down to clean his manhood carefully and knelt, kissing what was now clean and hard softly before washing his legs, stroking down and then up along them gently. When she was through, she wanted to take him into her mouth, but he took hold of her arms and pulled her up. He kissed her and brought her leg up, pressing himself between her thighs.

She welcomed the feel of him hard and firm as he penetrated her. April wanted to feel him deeper, and when he brought her other leg up, she wrapped them around his body. He held her hefty thighs and trust deeper into her and she felt alive and desirous. She kissed him passionately as he pressed her against the wall, seeking the depth of her, joining with her in their shared passion. When he pulsed into her, April took hold of his hair, gripping it between her fingers, reveling as he pushed still deeper into her.

When he was spent, he lowered her legs gently. April found them wobbly and weak, and stood under the warmth of the water, letting it pour energy back into them. Nigel kissed her again and pulled away, smiling as he dipped his head under the stream of water to wash his hair.

"I like showers," April said. She brought her own head under the showerhead and hoped that the water would mask her embarrassment over saying something so silly.

Nigel looked at her. "They can be very nice, when the company is."

A playfulness moved through April and she tilted her head to one side as she reached for shampoo. "I tried to be very nice and you stopped me."

Nigel laughed. "I didn't think that good girls were supposed to do that."

April's mind turned and spun at his teasing. "I'm in a shower with a man I just met yesterday. How good of a girl can I be?"

April's breath caught at the look in Nigel's eyes. It was both dark and desirous, and empathetic and sincere. She had no way to respond to it, and no word for the feeling it drew up inside her. She wanted to throw her arms around him and run away screaming at the same time. Overcome by her fear and desire, she could only stand there, her hands at her head, ready to massage shampoo into her scalp.

"You can be as good as you want to be," Nigel said.

He brought shampoo up to his own head and closed his eyes as he worked it through his hair. April swallowed hard and washed her own as well. When he opened his eyes again, the depth of emotion had passed. April suppressed a shiver and wondered once again at this man. He was a playboy. This week and this affair was one of many he had, one of many that he would have.

Some small part of her mind tried to challenge that, and April quashed it quickly as she rinsed her hair and turned off her side of the shower.

This was just an affair, just like any other Nigel Conroy had. He was taking a young woman he saw in distress and helping her through it the only way he knew how to. She bore him no ill will for that. In fact, April thought the world could use a few more Nigels.

****

The dining hall was lit brightly tonight, and a string quartet played Vivaldi as guests entered. Nigel led April to a table for two and they sat down, waiting patiently for a server to come by. Evening meals were meant to be more intimate, but the menu was still a general fare for all guests, a choice of steak, chicken, or fish, with either rice or potatoes and summer vegetables. April decided that she would have the fish and rice while Nigel ordered a steak and requested a bottle of wine to be brought out to them.

April spotted Leah among the servers and gave her a small wave. She did not want to embarrass Nigel, and while she thought he would understand her wanting to say hello to her friend, she knew that the other guests would consider the gesture to be gauche at best. Leah gave her a small and excited wave, looking from April to Nigel and back. She mouthed, "wow" as she poured water for another table, and moved to another. April gave an innocent shrug and smiled.

Nigel looked over his shoulder and back to April, smiling. "I think you've inspired new dreams in the female staff."

April laughed. "If only it were that easy for romance." She paused and thought about her last two days. "I'm not even sure how this happened."

Nigel reached under the table and brushed April's knee lightly. She could see he wanted to say something, but before he could, a man walked up to the table. Nigel withdrew his hand casually and looked up at the newcomer.

It took April a moment to register who the man was, and panic filled her. This was Chloe's father, and she could imagine the story told to him, and the reprimand her friend received. April had never met Michael Stuart, when she was hired on, she only worked with Mr. Graven, but she understood him to be a shrewd and clever businessman.

"Mr. Conroy, it is always a pleasure to have you here at the Estate." Mr. Stuart turned his attention to April and gave her a broad smile. "Ms. Edwards, it is good to see that you're enjoying your stay with Mr. Conroy. My daughter sends her regards."

April relaxed at the tone in Mr. Stuart's voice. Whatever story had gotten to his ears, it was either not believed, or countered, perhaps by Chloe herself. April made a note to herself. If she could not find her friend this summer, she would do so during the school year – assuming she was able to get back down to New York City to attend the university. "Thank you. Please tell Chloe I said hello."

Mr. Stuart nodded his head. "I will. She's enjoying a nice trip in Europe right now. She's spending the summer studying there as part of a fellowship. I will be sure to let her know when I talk to her. The both of you enjoy your evening."

He walked away from the table and over to another. April looked to Nigel to see him smiling wisely.

"What?" she asked.

"You looked like a deer caught in headlights for a moment there," Nigel said.

"The whole reason that I had a job here is because Chloe convinced her father to hire me. I was afraid that the worst of what happened reached him."

Nigel shook his head. The server brought their wine and poured a glass for each of them. When she left, leaving the bottle on the table between them, Nigel spoke. "I doubt anyone would have dared saying anything to him. The whole situation would have had him asking too many questions and probably getting other people not you fired. He probably wouldn't do anything to Worthington, though he should, but there are limits to what even Mr. Stuart can do."

April sipped her wine. She had not thought about just how precarious of a position that Mr. Graven really was in with how he had fired her and why. It occurred to her that she could file a complaint, but she realized she did not want to. Mr. Graven seemed to really care about his staff. His attitude toward her did not mask that. She doubted the scene would have played out quite the same way if it had been anyone else. The situation may have been hushed. The girl may even have been reassigned to other duties while Mr. Worthington was here. She thought that other things aggravated the situation, and while it was not right for Mr. Graven to hold her accountable for her father's actions; it was not worth him losing his job over.

"You're a good person," Nigel said.

April blushed, wondering if he read her mind, or if he just understood the situation itself. "Thank you."

"I mean it, you are." Nigel sipped his wine. "Anyway, I'm glad that you accepted my invitation."

"I am too."

They enjoyed their dinner together, using time to chat and get to know each other a little better. That tiny voice April's head tried to ask her if that was the kind of conversation that playboys engaged in, and she refused to answer. Her life was complicated, very complicated. She did not need to complicate someone else's as well.

After dinner, they wandered the estate house, seeing what festivities were taking place tonight. A company was holding an important shareholder meeting in one of the conference rooms. Both of them thought that was too boring to enjoy. Staff cleared the dining hall and the string quartet continued playing music. Guests who were not taking part in the shareholder meeting or any of the other smaller events filled up the dining hall, dancing to baroque music and enjoying the evening on the veranda.

April and Nigel joined in this. Nigel showed April a few simple steps for ballroom dancing, and they moved together to the music. With his arm around her waist, leading her in steps, April felt her desire swell up through her body again. She wanted to kiss him and knew that would not be proper here. They spotted the couple from the trail and exchanged smiles. As they danced past, April caught a snippet of their conversation and realized they were enjoying their anniversary here together.

"This is a magical place," April said as Nigel guided her off the dancefloor and over to a table where drinks were set out for guests.

"Oh?" Nigel handed her a glass of punch and looked at her curiously.

"The couple on the trail today, they're enjoying their anniversary here."

Nigel glanced out to the floor. "Is that so?"

"Apparently. I wonder how many other people are here for special occasions."

Nigel paused as he brought his glass to his lips and considered the people out on the dance floor. "I've never thought about it. I always just come up here and enjoy the mountains and the lake. I don't really think about what is going on with the rest of the guests unless I know them personally."

"I wonder about people sometimes," April said. "When I was a child, I would watch people on the street and wonder where they were going to and coming from. When we would be in a restaurant, I would imagine what conversations people were having at other tables. I always found my life to be easy and boring, so it was a fun way to make things interesting."

"Oh for things to be easy and boring."

April looked and saw Nigel's eyes turn dark with thought again. She supposed that for him, a boring life would have been ideal. She could not imagine what it would have been like for him. Did he have grandparents battle for custody of him, or did servants and lawyers raise him. He did not talk about that in the Playboy interview. April found herself curious again, and wondered if she would have the chance to explore that deep into him.

They danced for a few more songs before walking out onto the veranda and back up to Nigel's cabin. They held hands as they walked, taking in the view of the stars above them. April concentrated on trying to remember the names of any of the stars and constellations she saw and was ashamed that she could not. She should know them. She had learned about them in high school.

She never applied herself, and that knowledge drove home her precarious situation. She always assumed that he father's money would be there to take care of her. She would just move from that security to the security of a man. Now, that option was not open to her. She was not marriageable material. She was fine for a fling, but she did not want to live her life being the naughty fling of rich men.

She was going to have to decide on a direction for herself. She realized that depending on her mother was not the answer either. She was an adult. It was time that she acted it, and took on the responsibilities that brought.

Nigel let her into the cabin and followed her inside. He walked to the fireplace and turned on the gas starter. The logs, April realized, were only for show, to create a simulated fireplace. It was still beautiful, however, and she found herself pushing aside her thoughts and worries for another day.

She walked over to the couch and sat down. Nigel joined her and when he leaned close to her, April welcomed his kiss and his arms around her waist. She thought of making love to him in front of the fireplace and her excitement grew.

He broke the kiss and brought his hand up to April's cheek. She looked into Nigel's eyes and wondered at what thoughts were behind them. His eyes still looked contemplative and serious.

"I want you to stay with me," Nigel said.

April smiled. "I can sleep in your room if you'd like." She knew that was not what he meant, even as she said the words. She did not want to have the conversation that was coming. She realized that she had been running from it since their shower today and she thought she understood why now.

"That will be nice, but that's not what I mean," Nigel said.

April put her finger on his lips. He took her hand and kissed the back of it, bringing it back down to her lap.

"It is not fair," he said. "You're going through something you should not have to go through. Nothing that happened is your fault, but you're suffering for it."

"Lots of people suffer for things that aren't there fault." April suspected that Nigel suffered a lot. What was it actually like, growing up the son of a woman who killed herself and her husband? How many years did he spend wondering if that would happen to him? How many people treated him as if it would?

Nigel let out a sigh. "They do. I would help every single one of them if I could. We can't. We can only help those we can." He paused and sat back. "Do you know about what happened when I was a child?"

April nodded her head. "I read an interview where you talked some about it."

"The woman who took me out of the fire, she was my nanny. She was a kind woman. She was stern, and I grew up thinking she was mean sometimes. She took care of me. She did not have to stay with me. She could have let my family's lawyers find someone else. She was burned very badly in the fire. I lied when I told the interviewer I didn't remember the night very well. I did, but I didn't want to talk about it. She refused to let the paramedics treat her or take her to the hospital until she knew I was okay. She ended up being scarred very badly because of that, but it was the kind of woman she was. She stayed because I was the person she could help."

April took in a deep breath and squeezed Nigel's hand tightly.

"I want to help you. You were not working here because you wanted to. You were here because you had to be. No one should have to work like that. I don't want you to have to work like that."

April felt her heart filling and breaking at the same time. She cared about Nigel, more deeply and more quickly than she thought she would ever care about anyone. She could see herself easily falling in love with him, if she were not there already. She appreciated what he wanted to do, and she thought she understood what it meant to him.

That did not mean she could just accept it.

"Did you know I couldn't name a single constellation in the sky tonight?" April asked.

Nigel gave a small laugh. "I think I know the Big Dipper and Little Dipper. Not everyone knows the constellations."

"No, but people can point to the things they do know," April said. "I can't. My whole life I have depending on other people. I depended on my father to put me through school. I knew I just had to wait to get married and have another man to depend on for my livelihood. If it didn't work out, I would be able to get a nice alimony settlement and probably more money from Daddy again.

"I can't do that anymore. It doesn't matter that it's not fair. It matters that it life now. If I go back to school, I can get a real degree. I can figure out what I want to do with my life and do it, and not have to depend on anyone else."

Nigel brought his hand up to her cheek again. "It's a hard place, I know. The most important person in your life let you down, and depending on another person after that is scary. What happens if I let you down?"

April felt her heart break. She did not want to look at Nigel that way, but he was right. That was exactly what she was scared of. It was more than that, though. She could not expect him to pick up where others left off in taking care of her. It was not just a matter of what he might do anymore. It was what she had to do.

"You're such a wonderful person," April said. She leaned against the back cushion of the couch and let herself gaze into Nigel's eyes. "From most of the stories I've read about you, you're this carefree playboy who does philanthropy and just enjoys his money. You really are so much more than that. It's not that I think you would hurt me. I'm scared of it, but I know better. It's also what I have to do for me."

Nigel leaned his head against the back cushion and looked at her, silent in whatever contemplation he was in.

"I have no idea how I'm going to do this. A lot of people work their way through college. Some of them take student loans. I can do that too if I have to. If I talk to the financial counselors, they'll help me find a job and work out a schedule that I can pay for. I can always change schools if I need to. People do it every day. I'm no one special; I just thought I was for a long time."

Nigel let out a deep breath. She could see understanding and acceptance in his eyes.

"I could see you with a career. I think if you find something that you're passionate about, you could really put yourself into it and do something amazing," he said. "I would like to see that."

April smiled. "Thank you."

"Can I pay for school?" Nigel sat up again.

April was stunned and unsure how to answer his question. He had turned this around somehow and she felt as though she had been flipped on her head. "Pay for school?"

Nigel nodded. "I see the people who work their way through college. Sometimes they can pursue what they want. Sometimes they have to compromise. I want you to find and pursue whatever you want. I can pay for your school. You can stay on campus or with me, which ever you want. I won't pressure you there, though I would like to keep seeing you after this week."

April's mind was still trying to catch up to this strange change in their conversation. She tried to find words, and could not get anything to make sense from her mind to her mouth.

"You can say yes," Nigel said. "I would really like that."

April let out a laugh and sat up. She shook her head and looked down, trying to let her mind finish playing catch up. Nigel was serious about helping her. She did not think it was just some passing fancy of his. His understanding and his persistence told her how intent he was on this. She looked up and smiled at him. "Okay. But I get to pay you back for my school, even if I'm just donating it to your foundation. I appreciate it, but I want to be able to give something back to you."

Nigel returned her smile and broadened it. "I can accept that. You will have to apply yourself, though. I fully expect you to find a career that you can follow through on."

April moved closer to him on the couch. "I promise. I'll think about it this summer and decide." She paused before kissing him and pulled back. "What do I do during the summers?"

Nigel put his arms around her waist and pulled her down to him. "I'm sure we can negotiate something."

He kissed her. April welcomed his tongue through her lips. She thought again of making love to him in front of the fireplace and moved her hands up to unbutton his shirt.

It was a good place to start.

The Billionaire's Caregiver

People often think a new beginning is something that happens when there is a tragedy. Shelby Watson, on the other hand, disagrees entirely. Sometimes, a new beginning can simply happen to someone, and not be some epiphany out of the ashes of what was once a mess.

Simply put, life happens, but starting over is never easy. Shelby sighed and stretched out her legs on the sofa. Tomorrow, she would start again. Never one to be defeated, she knew she could pull herself out of this "new mess" she was in.

There was something about the way her big toe poked through the worn socks that made her rethink that idea entirely.

"You and me, Puppy Dobbs...she scooped up her puppy who had buried its head under the thick blanket. "All we really need is each other." Dobbs was a Chihuahua mix. Shelby found him by the door of her apartment one day, and when she opened her apartment door, he ran right in, in front of her.

He had been there since. It may have been the forlorn look he had about him that Shelby found endearing, or just the fact that he was standing there soaked to the bone. Whatever it was, Shelby knew she couldn't leave him out there, so let him stay.

The sound of banging caused Shelby to wince slightly. The pipes in this old building were always making some awful noise whenever someone was taking a shower. Shelby looked around at her efficiency apartment.

Clean and tidy it, was her home. She lived in the 3rd block of town. The lower the number indicated the worse sections of town. This was no exception. Her neighbors all consisted of drug dealers and prostitutes, though none unfriendly. Shelby would work early mornings and try to be home before dark. As long as she kept to herself nothing bad would happen to her...well less likely to, anyway.

All of the details of her life had changed now. The part-time morning job she had been able to find, she had lost. Nothing of her doing, simply a cut in positions at the senior home she was working at. They had pulled her aside that morning and given her the bad news.

"Shelby, your work here has always been wonderful. I hope you realize this is not a reflection on the quality of your work. It's simply based on the financial needs of the company." Dr. Brenner sighed and looked over at her as he delivered the news.

"Many of the seniors are moving into better equipped facilities and they...well they already have staff there. He ran his thin bony fingers through is even thinner hair.

It was obvious to Shelby this wasn't something he enjoyed doing and decided to help take the pressure off.

"I understand Dr. Brenner. I really do. I just don't know how I'm going to make it now." Life had always been a series of ups and downs for Shelby, and this was just one more set back. She stood to stand and extended her hand to Dr. Brenner.

"Thank you for helping me get things going here Dr. Brenner. The last three years have been wonderful. I hope you will let me use you for a reference." He stood and methodically pumped her hand, covering the hands with his other one.

"I really am sorry, Shelby."

There was a sense of helplessness that Shelby felt when she headed home. Now, she and her pup gracefully sat on the old worn sofa she had gotten from the thrift store down the street. Shelby decided it was time to start sorting the factors of her life out. She jumped up and grabbed her notebook from the counter.

Determined, she created her spreadsheet, lists of bills, things to do, what not to do, etc. Balancing her checkbook, Shelby calculated that she was ok for the next three weeks, but when the rent was due, she would be in trouble. She walked into her kitchen and pulled out a family-sized can of spaghetti from the cupboard, methodically putting it into a bowl and then the microwave. Her eating habits were terrible, but instead of trying to shed the extra 30 pounds she gained over the winter, she ate even more.

This is not where she envisioned herself a few years ago. She had big plans to go back to college to get her graduate degree in nursing. She was barely scraping by, but she knew that her resilience was powerful and that she would make it through. The one thing she was sure of was that she would not cry about it but would just keep moving on.

The next day things seemed bleak. Shelby walked to the corner store and bought a newspaper and began sifting through the want ads looking for a job. She wasn't above doing anything and would do whatever necessary to keep things going. Sitting on her foot, she took notice of anything related to her field first.

Under the dark header she saw an ad for a home health nurse. Perfect. She picked up the phone and called, but was greeted by a nasty voice.

"Kayla I told you I can't do this with you right now. You will just have to trust me. It's better this way." Shelby winced at the explosion.

"I'm sorry Sir. I think I may have the wrong number, I was calling about an ad." As she began to cradle the phone back into the receiver, she heard him yell.

"Wait yes, Oh God I'm an idiot. Miss...Miss?" He was obviously flustered.

"I'm here."

"Good. I'm terribly sorry. Your number was just like someone else's, and well... Ok, so yes, can you come out today? I need to wrap this up before I leave this weekend, and I have only gotten a few responses."

Encouraged, Shelby shot up out of her chair. "Yes, of course I can, what time?"

"Um, let me think." She heard shuffling on the other end. "How about now?"

"Now?" Shelby looked around mentally, figuring out what to wear." Sure now is good. I just need an address."

After getting all the necessary information, Shelby changed into a light grey dress and black boots. Shelby pulled her hair back and gathered up all of her references. As she started to walk out, she grabbed her purse and said a silent prayer.

"Wish me luck Dobbs, this is for dinner tonight."

Maneuvering her car down the highway was easy. Shelby loved road trips and had been into the town of Fauquier many times. Often considered the "rich" area, she never had much opportunity or reason to come this far out before.

Today was different. She had an interview, and hoped it would fix this mess she was in. Pulling down the long winding road into the countryside, Shelby admired the houses as she passed them. Most of them were old, and laced with gingerbread latticework. They looked warm and cozy. At the end of one street in particular, Shelby found the house she was looking for.

All she could do was stop the car and look up in awe. There is no way, she thought to herself. The magnificent mansion was on top of a ridge high above the roadway. There was a winding back entrance that was gated, and the front lawn was landscaped perfectly. Shelby glanced over at her car with it's rusted out fenders, and wondered if she really knew what she was doing.

With a sigh, she pushed her glasses back up and drove up the driveway. She pulled off to one side, straightening her dress as she stood and shut the door. She mentally prepared herself for whatever was on the other side of the door, took a deep breath, and knocked.

Billionaire Michael had never been more frustrated in his life. He was handling the merger of two companies, trying to line up a meeting with his partner, and simultaneously trying to find someone who could come sit with his grandmother. At 40, Michael was all business with dark hair and eyes and didn't have time for anything frivolous. His grandmother was his only soft spot. She had raised him, and her encouragement is what created the man he was now.

Suddenly ill, the doctors believed she had a stroke, and now she was in bed and unwilling to do anything. He glanced over at the clock. Where was this girl anyway? She seemed interested, but was probably another "no show." He started gathering up some paperwork just as there was a knock at the door.

Shelby waited patiently. When the door finally did open, she found herself stunned for a moment as she looked at the most handsome man she had ever met. Tall and dark, he was almost like a sculpture. Trying not to stare, she attempted to recover quickly.

"Hello, I'm Shelby. We spoke on the phone." She held out her hand to him.

Michael took her hand, shaking it lightly. He was not without his own reaction to her. Plain and overweight, she had hair piled on top of her head. It was dark brown and a nice accent to her almond-colored eyes. She wore little makeup but she was naturally pretty, she thought.

"I'm glad you're here, though I thought you would have been here sooner." Shelby frowned at the gruffness in his voice. He wasn't as pleasant as she had hoped.

"I'm sorry, I was coming from Manassas." She tried not to take offense, as he was obviously very busy.

"I see. I am looking for someone to care for my grandmother. Full-time and an occasional Saturday. I try to be here on weekends as often as I can, and she has another nurse as well. I need someone who can try to get her to do more, or at least want to. She had a stroke a month ago and the doctors think she should be fine to get out again, but she is simply laying there." He paused to look her over.

"You don't look as strong as I had hoped. Are you sure this is something you'd be interested in?"

Shelby felt the anger rise. "Mr. Jameson, I can assure you that I am very capable, despite your opinion of my large stature. Would it be possible for me to meet your grandmother? I think it's always important to see how well I click with someone."

"Sure that's fine. She knows you're coming. We can head upstairs in just a few moments. I'd like to ask a few more questions first, if that's ok?"

"Certainly." Shelby relaxed slightly. The fact that this guy was an ass made the fact that he was gorgeous much easier to look past.

"Ok, so I see you are working with Everest Healthcare. Do you plan to continue to do that as well?"

"If so, this may be a bad idea. I really need 100% attention for this. My grandmother is very important to me, and multitasking is something most people think they are good at, but sadly..." he looked her over once again, "are not."

Fuming, Shelby responded in clipped tones. "No, I am no longer there. I was let go recently." Before she could elaborate, Michael interjected quickly.

"Why? Was there some sort of horseplay or something? I won't tolerate any of that at all, Miss Watson. I simply won't. You do seem rather young, and I can understand if this is something that you don't feel you can handle."

He stood up as if he was dismissing her entirely.

Panic set in but even that wasn't enough to calm her anger. "Mr. Jameson, I have been working at this for a long time. I am not young, as you so nicely put it, and as a matter of fact, I'm 33. I love this type of work, and the reason I was let go was for budget cuts, not horseplay. Perhaps if you allowed people to answer your questions without simply writing them off, you would have more candidates for this position."

Shelby stood to leave.

Fire and ice. That was all he could think of. She was absolutely adorable when she was mad. He could see how her nose slightly turned red as she had been giving him a piece of her mind and although not used to being talked to like that, he gained a new kind of respect for her.

"Point taken, Miss Watson. Shall we go meet my grandmother?" He held the door to the hallway for her and allowed her to pass as he made his way up the stairs motioning for her to follow. Shelby was surprised she had even gotten this far. He was a real piece of work, this guy. Money did that to people, she thought, and could only assume that was it. Along the hallway there was artwork. Some bright, some dull, and some muted. It was a lot to take in. As they rounded the top of the stairs, Shelby looked down and couldn't help but think that her meager apartment would fit in the foyer below.

Nancy Jameson was in good spirits. She wanted to do more, but her body just wouldn't allow her to. Besides, when she is here like this, Michael comes around more. He was her only grandson and always had been her favorite.

She had three granddaughters, but they all had their own families, and were too busy to ever visit. Michael had always been special. He had dark coloring like his grandfather and was just as stubborn. She smiled warmly as Michael entered the room with a petite brunette in tow.

Nancy didn't miss the sparks that flew from the young lady's eyes as Michael made some comment on how he could show her how to use the elevator if need be.

"Grandmother this is ...I'm sorry what your name was again?" He did look guilty so Shelby took pity on him and extended her hand to Nancy.

"Hello, my name is Shelby, how are you?"

"Well I'm in this bed deary, so not very good, I suppose." She winked at Shelby and smiled wide.

"My grandson feels like he needs to find someone to watch over me and make me do things I am not ready to do. I suppose that's why you're here my dear. Come over here and let me get a look at you."

Having taken an immediate liking to Grandmother Nancy, Shelby complied and walked over towards the bed. Nancy noticed how her grandson followed Shelby's every move. This was interesting indeed and was exactly the distraction she needed!

After a while of discussion and rules, Shelby stood to leave. "It was very nice to meet you Miss Jameson."

"Now Dear, if you're going to be here with me all the time, I insist you call me Nancy or Grandmother, whatever suits you."

"Grandmother, no one has offered Miss Watson a job yet. I hardly think she needs to start calling you Grandmother." Michael chuckled.

"Michael Dear, it is my money is it not?" Grandmother smiled up at him lovingly and patted his hand on the bed. "So, I say she is hired."

"Shelby that is if you will take the job of course."

Never a person to have nothing to say, it took everything Shelby had not to laugh at the interplay. It would seem that Grandmother Nancy was the only one to bring Michael down a peg or two. If for that reason alone, Shelby would take the job.

"I would love to Nancy." Shelby smiled up at Nancy and then at Michael.

There was some mix of being irritated by his grandmother's words and being floored by the smile that Shelby gave him. He didn't know what to say. After clearing his throat, he kissed his grandmother on the head and turned to leave.

"Miss Watson, if you will kindly follow me back down stairs, we can go over pay and hours, and so on."

Shelby said her goodbyes again and followed Michael down the stairs. He even smelled good, like leather and soap. What was most adorable was the way his hair curled in the back of his neck just slightly. What in the world was wrong with her?

Never suckered in by the connection between men and women, she usually had a fairly good grasp on self-control. Sure she had met a few nice guys and done her share of dating, but that was a long time ago and there had been no one in at least three years. Maybe that was it, she needed to get out more.

Offering her a chair, Michael detailed the terms and pay of the job. More money than she could imagine, Shelby sat stunned while he rambled on.

"Miss Watson is that acceptable?" She glanced up at him sharply. Oh no, what had she missed.

"Yes of course, that's more than fair."

"When can you start?" He watched her closely. He could almost watch the play of emotions she was thinking and feeling.

"Anytime is fine. I don't live far, even if I was late today. So I am free anytime."

"I'm not sure if you realize that this job is more than just being here from one time to another. Obviously, you will have to move in here, as that is part of the deal." He moved to gather up his things and glanced at his watch. He was already late and was starting to get irritated, as this matter should have been handled over an hour ago.

"Oh no, I can't do that Mr. Jameson, I have my own place. I'll stay there." He was surprised. He had seen the worn shoes she was wearing, and heard the racket her poor car made as it climbed the hill to the house. He just assumed that she would be more than happy to move in.

"Suit yourself, but I may need you sleep over on occasion. Is that fair?" He caught her eye again and reached out to shake her hand.

He was all business and it suited him. She reached out and felt the warmth as he took her hand in his. She felt like he lingered perhaps just a second longer than normal; but it was probably just her imagination. There was something powerful about the way he carried himself. Like right now, just staring at her. Closing her eyes for a moment, she managed to get out "Of course."

After saying their goodbyes, Shelby made her way to the car and headed home. What was it about Michael Jameson that made her crazy? He was arrogant, stubborn and bossy. He was also handsome, loving to his grandmother, and made her feel safe. All of that from one visit. Thankfully, he didn't live in the house year round, or she would be in trouble for sure.

The next few months were a flurry of activity. Shelby commuted every day to her job with Nancy which she loved, and had enough money to pay up her rent for a while. Michael and she spoke on the phone almost every day discussing Grandmother's day and how things were going. He typically had a joke to tell, but on some days, he was distant and moody.

Either way, they had come a long way and she considered him a friend. Gone was the canned spaghetti, and Shelby was actually able to cook healthy food for herself. Even Dobbs was happier. She had just settled down to watch TV for a bit before turning in when the phone rang. It was a frantic Michael.

"Watson, my grandmother seems to have had a heart situation of some kind. I am in town and headed to the hospital and she has asked to see you." He was obviously in pain as he choked it out. Despite their differences, Michael had been nothing but nice with her and she didn't want to see him hurt. Worry was a motivator for Shelby and she immediately started to change clothes as he talked.

"..wanted to know if she had been acting differently lately or anything?"

"NO no, she's been fine, and we have actually been walking a few times and..."

He cut her off immediately. "You had her walking? What in the world, Watson were you thinking? She wasn't ready for that. Just come to the hospital as soon as you can." He hung up leaving Shelby stunned.

She was frustrated herself wondering if he was right. She gathered up her purse and headed downstairs. Trying to avoid the people in the halls, she made it to her car safely and let out a deep sigh. Unfortunately, it was not meant to be. As she turned the key nothing happened. Slowly, she laid her head on the steering wheel. What now? She jumped out to look under the hood. Apparently, sometime during the night, someone had stolen her battery... now she was stuck. Knowing she could never forgive herself if she didn't see Nancy, Shelby made her way back to her apartment and called him.

"Yes What!" He yelled into the phone.

"Michael, please don't yell at me."

"Oh, it's you. I'm sorry, Watson. The number thing again. Yes what's up?"

After much explaining, it was settled that Michael would come by and pick Shelby up on his way. She wasn't too far from the hospital herself but at night it was better to ride with someone. A few minutes later Shelby heard the knock on her door and opened it to a disheveled Michael. He was a mess, worry etched on his face, but handsome as ever.

Michael took in the apartment, if that's what you call it. Small but tidy, he imagined she could do just about everything. His issue was with her neighbors.

"This..is where you live, Shelby?" He gestured to the occupants sitting in the halls and the loud music.

"Yes why?" Shelby had her pride. This was her place and it wouldn't sit well if he was insulting.

"I'm terrified for my safety out there. I can't imagine how you've made it all this time. You're so vulnerable and there are at least 20 people just hanging outside."

"I am not so vulnerable and I am just fine. Let's go." She crammed her gloves into her purse and yanked open the door leaving it open so he could follow.

In the car Michael looked over at her. She had her signature bun in place and there was a pained look on her face. Obviously, he had hurt her feelings.

"Look Watson, I'm sorry. I didn't mean anything by it. I just worry. I mean grandmother worries about you is all." She had noticed the slip he made and smiled inwardly. He cared.

They arrived at the hospital and Nancy looked tired, but was noticeably happy to see her two favorite people. These two sure move slowly and I'm not getting any younger, she thought. She smiled at them both. What a striking couple they make. This little heart "issue" was just what was needed to bring them together for a while.

"Oh my dears, I'm so happy to see you both. They say I'm ok but are keeping me for a few days for observation. Can you imagine two whole days? I'll be bored out of my mind." Truthfully, she was glad. She had been feeling uncomfortable today but she knew Michael was coming to town and wanted he and Shelby to spend some time together.

"I'm just glad you're ok." Shelby was concerned at how pale she was. "This is my fault. We shouldn't have been walking this week."

"Oh pish posh. It's probably just gas or something." Michael rolled his eyes at his grandmother.

It was at that time that the nurse came in.

"I'm sorry, but you'll both have to get going Mrs. Jameson need to rest..."

They said their goodbyes and headed out front. Michael was very quiet, brooding again over some business merger gone wrong or something. She glanced over at him and he was caught up in thought, so she let the ride continue on in silence.

They pulled into her apartment complex and Shelby began to open the door.

"Wait, Watson I'm going up with you. I need to make sure you get in there in one piece."

"You don't have to do that Michael, I'm fine." She started walking and he followed anyway.

As they reached the top stairs of the building, a man reached over and touched Shelby on her leg making her jump. Michael immediately jumped.

"Don't touch her!" he moved between Shelby and the man.

"Michael it's fine. He is harmless." Secretly, she was touched that he jumped to her rescue.

Opening the door, they went inside. Michael was again impressed by the simple charm of her place. He sat down on the sofa and was greeted by a flying ball of fur. "Oh my, what is this?" He scruffed the dog on the back of the head and it bounced off.

"You once told me you had a dog but I hardly think that little thing qualifies, Watson." He smiled up at her.

Shelby had moved to the other end of the couch. "He is something, that's for sure." She giggled as they watched him get into a fight with a dog toy.

"You should just move into the house with us, Shelby." Hearing these words, Shelby caught her breath. She even noticed he had used her first name.

"Why would I do that? I'm perfectly fine here." What she didn't say was that she couldn't handle watching him with the various women he dated. She cared too much about Grandmother Nancy to ruin her relationship by being too close to him."

At that moment there was an obvious gunshot. Michael jumped up, and in his demanding voice she had grown to love he simply stated, "Get some things, Watson you're going with me."

The ride to the house was uneventful. Shelby knew he was mad, but to be honest, she wasn't sure why. He parked his car in front of the house and they went inside together. "You can have the room down here. I'll sleep upstairs and you know your way around. I'm getting a drink, I certainly need it."

She could use one herself, she thought as she went into the spare room downstairs. Changing into pajamas, letting her hair down, and tucking Dobbs into the bed, Shelby decided to go into the den where Michael was and get that drink. If, for any other reason but to calm her nerves. Knowing they were here alone was setting her on edge.

He was sitting in the leather-bound chair by the fireplace. He already had a drink, or was it two? Nothing could prepare him for her entrance. It felt like someone had punched him in the stomach. She was in all pink and her hair was flowing down her back. This casual image of her was one he had played out in his mind during one of their conversations on the phone. He had thought about it ...and now here it was.

He watched her walk over to the bar, pour a drink for herself, and tip it back. Impressive he thought. He stood up and moved closer to her. He could see all the shades of auburn in her hair when he was up close like this, she smelled like honeysuckle.

"You're moving in here, Watson." He said it with a finality that only made her angry.

"You can't tell me what to do, Michael. I work for you, but you don't own me." She was flushed with anger as he turned towards her.

"You could be killed, Watson. That place is dangerous, men groping you in the halls and gunshot...real actual gunshot, Watson." He ran his hand though his hair.

"My grandmother would kill me if anything happened to you and I didn't try and stop it." She couldn't help but feel some disappointment at the words. She had hoped he would say something about how he cared.

"I'm not moving in Michael. Let it go." She put her glass down and turned to leave. He grabbed her left arm and spun her around. It could have been the alcohol or the stress of the day, but something made him lose himself in that moment.

He gripped her wrist tighter than he meant to and put his right hand into the waves of her hair, pulling her towards him. The kiss had meant to be angry. He needed her to listen to reason but what started out hard, became softer, deeper, and more meaningful. Slowly, he dropped her other wrist and cupped her face in his hands, nipping at her lips and taking in the smell of her skin. When the kiss broke, he looked up at her.

"Watson, you're driving me crazy." He dropped his hands back down and watched the emotions play out on her face. Rocked to her core, Shelby could only stand and wait. Wait for the fluttering to subside, wait for her heart to stop racing, and wait for him to stop looking at her so intently. Not knowing what to say, she turned and walked stiffly back into her room. He followed her.

"Talk to me Watson. Why are you running from me? I know you feel this craziness just like I do."

"Yes I do Michael and that's why I won't live here." She turned to look at him. "I am a mess inside and I need you to go and leave me be so I can think straight." She saw the pained look on his face but heard him leave the room.

Shelby laid in bed thinking about that kiss. His kiss only intensified the connection they had. It wasn't all her. That was comforting, but what wasn't, was that she couldn't stop the fluttering she felt deep down. The way he moved towards her and the way he kissed deeply and without thought.

Laying here was obviously not going to figure it all out. She decided to go get a drink of water. They came from such different worlds. He always had someone worldly, gorgeous, and thin on his arm, some debutante. She had even met a few of them when he was there and she had been working.

The one thing they all had in common was that they were beautiful. Always regal and classy, she always found something to do to keep away from them. After they would leave, Grandmother Nancy always had some snide comment about each one that made Shelby giggle.

"He will never find the right one unless he shops from a different field," she would say. Smiling now, Shelby opened the refrigerator door and started sifting through things until she found exactly what she wanted. Cake, it was the best cake around and had been left over from a party Grandmother Nancy had earlier that week. She stood there eating quietly, not hearing him until he spoke.

"You have quite the "strictly business" thing going on here, Watson."

She slammed the door shut on impulse, having been caught red handed.

"Yeah, I try." She smiled slightly. He walked over to her and with one finger, wiped the chocolate off her bottom lip.

Feeling the heat begin to creep up again, Shelby took a step back.

"We need to talk Watson, and now." He walked until she had backed up to the bar. He moved his face closer to hers.

"I think it's obvious that I want you. I don't know how else to put it." The bluntness of the statement made Shelby gasp.

"The only way I'm going to stop trying is if you tell me you don't feel the same way." She was pinned between him and the bar and he was watching her face.

"Michael let me go," she tried to squirm but it was no use. She was stuck.

"Just tell me you don't want me to touch you and I'll leave you alone Watson. Just say it."

Knowing full well she felt the same way he did she, Shelby did the only thing she thought was right. She looked up at him and ran her finger down the right side of his face.

"I can't tell you any of that, Michael because I want the same thing." Before she could finish the words, he crushed his mouth to hers. He put his hands in her hair tilting her head back more. She kissed him back more fervently, having let go now. He lifted her up off the floor and put her on the bar top. Running his hands along her legs, all the while teasing and nipping her bottom lip.

"We should stop Michael." It was more of a pant than a statement.

"You're right, Watson, we should, but I can't. Not anymore." Pulling her to him, he lifted and carried her into the bedroom and kicked the door shut behind him. Sitting her down, she stood motionless, watching him take his shirt off and move towards her. She was frozen to the spot she stood on, not knowing what to do next.

He walked to her and started slowly unbuttoning the front of her pajamas. Each button exposed new skin that he had to kiss. He loved the way she smelled of sunshine and honeysuckle. He looked up at her.

Needing no words, she walked backwards towards the bed, pulling him with her as they went. Sliding back onto the comforter, he followed, pressing the length of him against her body. He looked down and knew in that moment, he was lost. Her hair spilled across the pillow, her lips were parted slightly from being thoroughly kissed, and her eyes were shining up at him. He could tell she was scared and excited. He ran his finger along her bottom lip.

"I need to hear you say it, Shelby. I need us to be real in this moment and together."

He gazed at her. "I can stop if you want, but you need to tell me now before I can't anymore." His honestly made her want him even more. She slowly pulled her shirt off and tossed it to the floor.

"I want you Michael, I always have." Needing no further encouragement, Michael stood and took off the rest of his clothes looking down. He stood back for a moment, letting himself take in her naked form. She was perfect.

Once, he thought her too big, but looking at her now, he adored every curve she was given. Almost scared to touch her, she made the move first.

"I'm getting a little self-conscious Michael. What's wrong with me?" She started to cover up again.

"No don't "...he grabbed her hand. "You're beautiful, Watson, absolutely beautiful." He laid down on the bed again, taking a moment to calm his racing heart. He was acting like a teenage school boy, wondering why in the world was so nervous.

This was different. He knew it and probably always had, but he needed her to feel loved, wanted, and cherished.

The night progressed, and the two made love into the early hours of dawn. Before falling asleep, the last thing she heard was him saying her name and draping one arm across her body. Sometime during the night, Shelby got cold, having been woken up by something, only to find herself naked as the day she was born. She tried to keep from moving, but right before she almost fell asleep, she felt Michael's arm grasp her stomach and pull her into him. He kissed her ear and they drifted back to sleep for a few more hours.

Never a late sleeper, Michael woke up to greet the day with a smile on his face. Shelby was amazing. She was not just beautiful to him, she a heart to match. She gave as much as she received, and never held back. This was something Michael couldn't help but admire. He looked at her lying among the sheets as he headed upstairs to shower and get ready for the day. He just didn't have the heart to wake her up.

Shelby woke up to the smells of coffee and the clink of pans. She rolled over to snuggle in more and her eyes flew open as she remembered...everything. Oh wow she had never been so careless in her life. She scrambled to jump in the shower before he found her. Before she was soaped up she heard him come into the bathroom.

"Watson, I see you're joining me today finally." He chuckled.

"Michael really, I am in the shower, I'll be right out." She could only smile as she heard him hum a tune as he left.

What would she do now? It had happened and there was no going back, but she could stop it now. Now that they had gotten it out of their system, she could put Michael Jameson out of her mind altogether.

She entered the kitchen, dressed for the day and ready to go to the hospital. Michael was cheery and leaned towards her as if to get a kiss. She managed to avoid it discretely.

Frowning, Michael went back to cooking. Something was wrong. Breakfast passed with no mishaps and they set off for the hospital.

Grandmother was overjoyed to see them. They each took a side and listened to her tell them about how awful the night had been and the bed situation. She moved on to complain about the food and how happy she would be at home. She could tell something was amiss between the couple, but it would sort itself out.

Michael was having a hard time understanding what Shelby was thinking. The night had been something people only dream about and yet when he got close to her, she ran. Something wasn't right, but he would find out soon enough.

The doctors came in and discussed the grandmother's situation. They equated it to a chemical reaction to something she ate, at which grandmother smiled. They passed the morning laughing with her, planning the next event. At lunch, the doctors ordered them out, saying she needed her rest, so the couple decided to go to a nearby restaurant for something to eat.

It was a beautiful café, overlooking a pond and situated amongst lush landscaping. They dined on wine and oysters, which were new to Shelby. Michael was about to broach the subject plaguing him, when a woman came up to the table.

"Michael darling, where have you been?" The woman was like something from the cover of a magazine. She had on long flowing pants and a silk shirt complete with a huge brimmed hat.

"Baby, I have missed you so much. How nice of you to bring the maid to lunch." She smiled over at Shelby, who immediately excused herself and went outside.

Angry Michael pushed the woman back away from him. "I told you to leave me alone. Why are you here? Stop calling me and stop following me."

Without waiting for an answer, he stormed out onto the street and to his car. Shelby was standing by the passenger side and he opened the door, then went to his side and got in.

"I'm sorry, Watson that was ...the number..." at her confused look he added "remember when you would call and I thought it was her?"

"Aha, that is her." Shelby still felt awful about the exchange and self-conscious as well. The maid, really?

When they arrived at the house, Shelby went to her room. Thinking she would have some time to think, she was surprised when Michael stormed in behind her.

"What the hell Shelby, after last night I thought,"

"What...you thought we would just act like nothing happened? You think I would go away? Well I'm not. I love Grandmother Nancy and I'm not going anywhere."

"What are you talking about Shelby? I don't want you to go anywhere. I want you here. With me." He said it with such finality, Shelby could do no more than look up at him.

"What?"

"I love you, Shelby. I have since the day we met and you came here. But when I was at your place and heard that gunshot it was all I could do to not kidnap you myself and tie you up here so I could keep you safe."

"But I'm not like you Michael. She called me "the maid" for goodness sake." She looked down for a moment.

"Shelby do you really think I care one moment about what people think?" I want you and I choose you."

Tears were flowing freely now as Shelby looked up at him.

"Well," He asked impatiently.

"Well what? " She was confused.

"Damn it Shelby, you're killing me. Do you or do you not feel anything for me?"

Laughing, she ran into his arms and kissed him. "Michael I have loved you from the moment you opened that door."

He let out an audible sigh. Happy and content, he pulled her close to him and kissed her deeply.

Hand in hand they headed back to the hospital. Grandmother had taken a nap and was refreshed as she looked out the windows to the parking lot. Seeing Michael, she smiled. He really was a good boy. But what made her happiest was seeing him hand in hand with Shelby.

Perhaps her plan had worked after all, and if she played it just right, she could somehow start planning a Fall wedding at the house. She may be getting old, but this was enough to keep her busy for at least a good many years to come.

The Billionaire's Wish

Braden Davenport was on cloud nine. Even now, as he pulled off his helmet, he felt great. He was on a streak and this was going to be his best season yet. He brushed his hand through his jet black hair and smiled at the people around him. It was nice having fans. They were the only constant in his life, always there to cheer him on. The problem was, they didn't really know him.

That's not to say that it isn't great doing what you love for a living. He was able to buy his first house at the age of 23, and at 29, he owned three. He liked to have a nice place to stay whenever he was in his favorite places. Racing was a dangerous sport, but it was in his blood, a part of him. Being here in Austin for the MotoGP race had been a fluke, but a happy one. He was a last minute add in and he was happy he said yes.

He would always rather be racing than home alone or out with some nameless girl that didn't know him very well. For now, he was home in Texas, at least for the next two months. It was the place where this all began and he was happy to be there. He loved the dry air and the open grounds in the hill country, and the city life in Austin. His next race was in Vegas and he was happy for the break. The win today would put enough money in the bank that he could live off forever, but it was never enough. Having lived such a hard life growing up, he liked the better, secure, lifestyle he had now.

He basically lived his life in an orphanage. He never knew his father, who left his mother soon after he was born. His mother was heartbroken and soon became an addict. He still remembered what it was like finding her there when he was 7. She made the wrong person mad, and they gave her some bad stuff. He found her unresponsive, lying on the living room floor. They didn't have a phone, but fortunately he was able to run to a neighbor and they called the police for him. He still carried around the guilt because he couldn't save her.

He eventually left the orphanage and made a few friends. He had a difficult time trusting people, getting close to anyone.

He got his first job at the thrift store in town. He learned the hard way that life was about making the right choices or you end up with nothing. Over time, he managed to secure a room, and that's when he met Gerald and Abbie Smith. Older, they were frequent shoppers where he worked, and they always amused him. At 80, Gerald was a big bear of a man. Abbie was a tiny little thing at 77. Abbie would tell Braden he looked too thin, and Gerald would pull him aside and talk cars with him, something he always loved. After a year or so, they invited him to dinner. At 19, he still seemed like a kid to Abbie. She was always fussing over him and making sure he actually ate when he came over.

Gerald was the person who taught Braden to race. He owned many bikes, he was a collector of sorts, and the moment Braden rode one, his life changed. He maneuvered them like a pro. After some help from Gerald's contacts, he quickly became successful and was able to secure himself a lucrative future in racing. When Braden was 21, Gerald passed away, and Abbie followed a year later. He moved in to help her after Gerald's passing, and held her hand when she died.

That was seven years ago now, and he could still remember it like it was yesterday. He shook his head, remembering, and smiled. He made sure his bike was always in tip top shape, and made frequent visits to his trusted mechanic and best friend, Mike's house. They met in his early years of racing, and had been friends ever since.

The most important thing that Gerald taught Braden was that the bike is your money and the only way you can ride it safely is if you have a hand in what goes on with it. The bike was his family, and he protected it as such. He finally set off for the hour drive to Marble Falls, where Mike lived.

Mike was always a party guy. One girl to the next and one disaster away from an addiction. What he did have was a nice house, and a serious garage behind it. It was the one thing he always took care of. His mother would come over once a month and clean up for him. As he pulled into the parking lot of the townhouses, Braden noticed the changes. The place next door was vacant the last time he was there, and he wondered if Mike even knew that someone had moved in.

He was taking the next few weeks to run off with his newest girlfriend and had given Braden the key so that he could drop some things off, and pick up some things for the bike. He noticed her the moment he pulled up. He watched amused as a woman was desperately trying to get her key to work in her door knob.

"Damn it."

She was angry and she was beautiful. She finally kicked the door and turned to go to her car. She stopped when she saw him watching her. She gave him a half smile before pushing her hair back and squaring her shoulder.

"I'm not usually so easily flustered. My key broke off in the door... now I am rambling sorry... so yeah, I should go." She turned to go again and he finally said something.

"I can probably get that out of there if you want me to try." He crossed his arms as she gave him a half smile.

"That would be... well... yes, please." She smiled at him again and he went to the truck.

Chloe closed her eyes and took a deep breath. She was standing here rambling like an idiot. It always happened when she met a guy, especially an attractive one. Attractive didn't even begin to describe this one. He was, by far, the most attractive guy she had seen in a long time. He had black hair and dark eyes and just enough stubble on his face to give him that mysterious look. She never even kissed a guy like that and she never would. It certainly didn't hurt to watch him though. He was all muscle, and it was obvious he worked out. She blushed as he came back towards her, hopefully he hadn't seen her looking him over like that.

He smiled as he worked on the door. She was looking him over and it made him smile. The fact that she blushed when he looked at her made him like her even more. He finally broke the broken key out and he turned to look at her again. It was her eyes that struck him first. Deep blue and full of life, they contrasted the abundance of red flowing hair. She was a big girl, he liked that about her. She had curves in all of the right placed and he wanted to touch every single one of them. He glanced at her hand and didn't see a ring, which was a good first step. He handed her the broken pieces of the key, and when his eyes met hers, he saw her blush again.

"It should be fine now, I had to put some lube in it." He gave her a half smile.

"What... oh thanks." She gathered the pieces up and headed towards the door. "Thanks again..."

"Braden... my name is Braden." He held his hand out to her and she shook it.

"I'm Chloe, nice to meet you."

"Perhaps I can get you to have dinner with me sometime, Chloe?" He watched the myriad of emotions cross her face.

"Sure, that sounds like fun." She turned to head back in again and he smiled.

"Chloe, can I get your number?"

"Oh, sorry." She wrote it down and turned to go again.

She was a flighty one, but that was part of the excitement for him. He watched her go inside and he left, heading for his place in the hills. She was timid, something he would remedy. Even now he thought about her curves and how they would feel under his fingers. He rarely ever lost at this and he didn't intend to start now.

Chloe shut the door with a thud. That was very sweet of him, offering to have dinner with him. It was typical of some guys, nicer ones anyway, to offer to take the big girl out. She didn't need to get paraded around and everyone's opinion of him go up because he did her a favor. Still, he seemed genuine. She made her way into the house and took a good long look at herself in the mirror. She had been working hard to lose weight, to be in better shape. She was down 20 pounds but she still hated the way she looked. Aside from her friends and her little brother, she was alone. In some ways it suited her. She'd had one serious relationship and that left her ready to just put the idea of love and romance behind her for good.

After, she made her way into her room to throw on pajamas and spent the rest of the afternoon cleaning until Charlie got out of school. At 12, he was more than a handful of energy. In a week, he would be gone with friends on vacation, and she would really be alone all summer. He had been living with her a year and a half now, but some days it seemed like only yesterday that he had moved in. She was 22 and ready to tackle the world when she got the call. Her parents and her little brother were in an accident.

Like most people, she didn't think anything could happen to her. She rushed to the hospital, but her parents were both gone, leaving Charlie, with her. It was a rough start, but they were good now. She'd be lying if she said she didn't get lonely sometimes though. He kept her busy, one activity to another. Motherhood at her age was not part of her plan, but she was lucky they had each other. That thought brought her back to Braden. She wondered if he had a family. He seemed like a nice guy.

She never had an opportunity to meet her neighbor. As far as she knew the little lady that came in and out on occasion was the only one who visited that house at all. She sighed, she had rambled on and on about nothing, he must have thought her a complete idiot. Finally, she sat down to calculate how to pull off everything this month.

She was a local teacher, well she was a substitute. She was still in school part-time but she was determined to finish. Most of the time she worked enough days to just barely pay the bills, but having a 12 year old with numerous after school activities put a dent in things. Not to mention the rent on this place was out outrageous. Since her parents were renting as well, their place was too much for her to take on.

They were always like the traveling circus, always moving and changing. Chloe didn't want that for her little brother. She lived that life and he needed stability. She would simply have to cut out some things, but first she would have to find what those things were.

Braden walked into his house, well Gerald's and Abbie's house. They left it for him in the will. No children of their own, they took him in and loved him as if he were theirs. He didn't live here, it didn't feel like he should, and to be honest, he didn't want to take over. He liked being able to walk in and see their things as they left it. It gave him a sense of peace. Deep down, he knew it wasn't healthy, he should sell it, but for now he couldn't let go.

He checked on things here and then headed to the place he lived in the hills. He called ahead the week before so that it could be opened up and aired out. He hadn't been here in months and knowing it would be ready was one of the many luxuries he enjoyed. He had a house manager and a housekeeper, both trustworthy friends, and he compensated them well for the work they did for him.

Once he was there, he made his way inside and he poured himself a drink, leisurely making his way to the large windows overlooking the city. He wanted her. The thought crossed his mind and he smiled. Chloe, there was something about her that struck a nerve, and he wanted to figure it out. He thought at first it had been her coy and shy personality, but he had played that game before and knew that wasn't it.

There was a depth to her, and he wanted to know more. Women were always around, throwing themselves at him and offering him their charms. It came with the business... and the money. It was rare he felt connected to someone who didn't know about either of those things. She felt the connection too, but she simply dismissed it, and he wanted to know why. He suddenly smiled as an idea came to mind. She had no clue who he was or the money he made. Even in her wildest dream, would she ever guess that he was a billionaire. He pulled out his phone and called Mike.

Braden pulled up to Mike's townhouse once more with a renewed spirit. Mike had given him the green light at least for the next few weeks. That would be plenty of time to figure Chloe out. He glanced over at her place before heading inside. Much like his penthouse, the place hadn't been lived in in months. Everything shined and gleamed. "Thank you Mrs. Anderson." He said under his breath.

She was a sweet woman, often quiet and reserved, but she could clean the hell out of this bachelor pad. He decided there was no time like the present to start pursuing his curvy neighbor. He made his way over to her door. It wasn't late, so he gave it a knock. She opened the door in a flurry, and as soon as she saw him, she looked shocked.

"Braden hello." She smiled at him and he felt the heat rising in him. Her hair was pulled up on top of her head and she was wearing a t-shirt and sweats. Casual and damn near the sexiest thing he had ever seen.

"Hello Chloe, thought I'd see if you were up for a chat? It's just that I've been out of town and it's hard to get resettled." He gave her a smile and gauged her reaction.

She was just a little intimidated. She assumed he would move on and let her be, but here he was, in his tight jeans and arms that looked ready to rip out of his shirt. She gulped slightly, what was wrong with her? She usually had more control over herself than this. She gave him a half smile.

"I wish I could. It's just that my little brother is here and is sleeping." There, that should put him off.

"Oh, I see. Maybe we could sit on the deck?" He shoved his hands in his pockets and she mechanically nodded a yes. He smiled at her again and she moved to let him in.

She must be completely out of her mind. What was she doing? She didn't even know him that well and she just let him walk right into her house. He could be a crazy person or something. She sighed.

"I'm not a killer or anything, if that's what you're worried about." They had made it to the sliding door and he leaned in behind her, whispering it in her ear.

She felt the heat of his breath on her ear and shivered. It had been a long time, very long, and she was just sensitive that's all. They moved out to the deck, and as she shut the door and turned towards him, he was directly in front of her.

"Are you married Chloe?" He leaned towards her as he said it, propping his arm against the sliding door beside her head.

"You're very forward aren't you?" "No, I'm not, said Braden, are you?" She ducked through his arm and made her way over to the wrought iron chairs on the deck. It was dark out there. Having forgotten the deck lights were blown, she silently cursed. She turned around again, and this time he walked over to the rail. She joined him there, waiting and suddenly he turned towards her.

"No, I'm not." He put an arm on either side of her and rested against the railing. As he did so he leaned into her breathing in the scent of jasmine.

She was lost in that moment, He was inches away from her and her only thought was that he must be really desperate to be here with her. More than anything else, she didn't want to look like a fool, it's happened before and she didn't want to go through that again. She dipped below his arm and faced the trees again. She could hear his chuckle, and she frowned.

"You are something else Chloe, you know I want to kiss you, but you keep running, why?"

She looked at him, surprised by his admission. "Why do you want to kiss me? I'm sure you have plenty of other women to kiss, besides, I don't even know you, Braden."

"What better way to get to know me, Chloe." He stood and gave her a smile.

There was something about the way he said it that left her wondering if he was serious or simply out of his mind. She shook her head and turned back around.
"Don't be ridiculous Braden."
She said it simply and he realized she meant it. He frowned as he thought about it. Maybe she wasn't attracted to him. There was only one way to find out. He slid over to the right and grasped her hand in his and pulled her towards him. He saw the look of surprise on her face as he put his hand against the back of her head, pulling her into his arms as his mouth crushed hers.
She was on fire and he did nothing but add fuel to it. She felt his mouth nip at her lips and then dive deeper. She opened her mouth to

him, unconsciously meeting his kiss eagerly. As their tongues danced, she felt the fire inside begin to build and grow. It had been so long, and he was very good. She felt his hands then start to move. First, slowly he ran them down her back and over the curve of her hip, pulling her even closer to him. She felt his mouth slowly leave her lips and trail down her neck and he nipped her collarbone. He moved his hands up her hips and his mouth found her again. The kiss was passionate and full of promise. She felt his hand slip under her shirt and she panicked, pushing him away.

Braden stood frozen, what the hell was wrong with him. He planned on sweet talking... maybe steal a kiss, but this... He ran his hand through his hair and walked to the deck to calm himself. One thing was for sure. She wanted him just as badly as he wanted her, she couldn't deny that now. He looked over at her, she was stone-faced and looked almost sad. He frowned, that was not what he expected to happen, but why would it make her sad?

"Chloe, I'm sorry." I didn't mean to get so carried away." She looked down and then back up at him, a smile now sitting on her face.

"I understand. Like you said, you haven't been home in months. I'm sure you're just tired." She moved to walk back to the door leading to the house. She whispered to herself "Plus it's dark out here, I'm sure that helps."

"Helps with what?" He was beside her, he was like a cat the way he moved.

"Nothing sorry, just rambling as always. I should get to bed, I have to be at work early." She smiled at him, but he knew something was wrong here.

"Sure, I understand." He turned to go and then spun back to look at her. "I like kissing you, Chloe. I won't lie about it, and in fact, I want much more than that. I wanted you to know I plan on trying to make sure you know that regularly." He walked down the front steps whistling. She stayed there until she heard his door shut. She leaned her back against the door to try and calm her racing heart.

The days went by quickly, they would often pass each other in the front yards or as they came home. Both of them caught up in work. He consistently asked her to come over for dinner, but she always had reason to say no. He never made any other move to kiss her or otherwise, and she relaxed more around him. They spent two different afternoons sitting out front talking about life, where each time she was sure they had an audience at all times. One afternoon she opened up more than she planned.

"So, Charlie?" Braden asked as Charlie was throwing a ball with a friend in the parking lot.

"My parents were killed in an accident, he was with them, but survived. That was almost two years ago now." She watched Charlie playing. "He is a good boy though."

"That has to be hard on you, suddenly having a 12 year old." Braden watched the expressions changing on her face.

"It took some adjusting, for all of us." She took a sip of water from her glass.

"Why aren't you married?" He asked it very matter of factly, but with a deeper tone to his voice. She turned to look at him.

"I almost was once, actually."

He sat up at her admission. So she had loved someone, being close to them. "You know you have to tell me now Chloe?"

"No, I don't Braden." She stood up, brushing off her skirt as she did and headed into her house. He stood and followed.

She noticed him standing in the doorway. "Really Braden, following me into my own home? Even for you that's a bit much." She started folding the towels on the table in the kitchen. He didn't say anything, but methodically started helping. She paused to look at him and he simply grinned at her. She rolled her eyes.

When they were done, he finally spoke. "Why don't you want to talk about it?"

She put her right hand on her hip. "Because it doesn't matter Braden, that's why." As she turned to go he grabbed her forearm and pulled her to him.

"It does matter Chloe, it certainly is part of why you are the way you are."

"What the hell does that mean "the way I am"?" She felt the sting then. She was different. Why did people always feel the need to point it out to her?

"Wait a minute Chloe what do you think I am talking about here?" He took another step closer, never letting go of her arm.

"Let me go Braden." Her eyes glittered dangerously.

"Not until you tell me."

"Fine." She yanked her arm free. "I was engaged, he seemed to accept me." She gave him a glance. "He was always sweet and kind and then when my parents died, he never made it to the funeral. He apologized, and I was stupid enough to believe him. When Charlie moved in, he tried to force me to send him away to a boarding school of some kind.

He said this was not the future he planned and that Charlie was not his problem. So I refused, and he slept with my friend. I caught them in my friend's house. The worst part was, it had been going on for a long time. She was one of those model-thin blondes. I should have known better." She looked over at him finally and he was in shock. He moved towards her again and she stepped back.

"I'm sorry that happened to you Chloe, he was an ass."

"Thanks."

Her voice was clipped and short now. He knew she was reliving it and it was his fault. He looked at her, she was sad and hurting and it had left something scarred in her. He felt that same feeling when he was put in that home. Like no one understood him or cared to. He didn't want that for her, for her to feel that way. He reached out and grabbed her again and pulled her to him. They stayed that way for a long time, just standing close with him pressed against her until Charlie came running in breaking the spell.

"Chloe, look what I found, a frog!" He happily made his way over to her and she shrieked backing up.

Charlie glanced at Braden, rolling his eyes. "Girls." Braden couldn't help but laugh at the scene before him.

"Well, I have to get going, Chloe. I expect to finish this conversation later." He ruffled his hand in Charlie's hair. "You be nice to your sister." He gave him a smile and he headed out. He had a tremendous amount of paperwork to sort through at his place.

The next week went by uneventfully. She would glance at his place when she went to work, subconsciously hoping to see him. He was a good friend of Charlie, and that was all. School would be out in two days. Finally, it was Saturday, and Charlie was leaving. She knew the Bakers were picking him up at 11 and she started helping him to move his things outside as they waited. He was smiling at her and she finally asked him why.

"You are gonna have a whole lot of time to spend with your new boyfriend next door when I am gone, Sis." He started laughing. She swatted at him.

"Charlie, that's not funny. Keep your voice down. He is not my boyfriend, he is our neighbor."

"Okay, so why is he always asking you out?" He looked up at her and started to laugh again.

"I don't know. Maybe he feels sorry for me because my little brother has such a big mouth." She pushed him as she made her way down the stairs.

"No, he likes you Chloe, I like girls at school... that's how he looks at you." He shrugged at her glare and went back to moving things.

"No, he doesn't, guys like him don't like girls... well like me. That's just the way the world is. It's up to younger guys like you to make the world better." She threw a pillow at him and he scrambled to catch it before it hit the ground. Finally, they noticed the Bakers coming up the side street, and after some time, he was loaded and leaving.

She waved at him, feeling a little sad at the prospect of spending so much time alone. Once it had been easy to fill her time, and now, she was like a mom, and without him, she wasn't sure what to do. She turned around and Braden was there watching her. She gave him a wave and headed back to her house.

He watched her go. It was the longest week of his life and all he wanted to do was touch her. Between issues with the races, complaints from other drivers about a leak, and his manager trying to set him up on random surprise dates at dinner time, he just wanted something normal. He wanted her. He heard what she said and it made sense to him now. "Guys like him and girls like her." She had no idea what he wanted, but he was going to tell her. He took long strides to her door and rang the bell. He felt the anticipation curling up. When she opened the door, he practically fell through it.

"Braden hello..." He cut her off, pulling her to him and covering her mouth with his. He bruised her lips with his attack and she felt her defenses slip away. She thought of nothing but him for a week.

They moved together in the living room and she leaned back on the couch as he pushed her down. She felt the length of him against her and it was perfect. His hands were everywhere and as he unbuttoned her shirt he felt her freeze.

"Look at me Chloe. I want you, all of you just as you are. Stop fighting me." She was still frozen and he knew he had to convince her. He pinned both of her arms above her head with his left arm as he moved his right hand over her curves. She was rounded and smooth, and he loved it. She was aware of every nerve ending in her body, as his hands reached around and under each breast, lifting her bra slightly so that the nipples were exposed. He cupped each globe lovingly until he reached the pert nipple that had hardened under his touch. He pulled and tugged on them, creating a deep ache deep down, soon covering each one in succession with his mouth.

Chloe was lost in the sensation. No one had ever taken time with her like this, ever. His hands were lighting her on fire with every movement.

She was all fire, just like he knew she would be. He was almost in pain with the need to rip off her clothes and bury himself inside her, but he wanted to go slow, wanted it to be good for her too. She was laid out on the couch, her hair, a red flaming swirl around her head and yet he could still tell she was nervous. He moved lower to make a final step in making her his.

Her eyes flew open as she felt him slide his hand under her and lift her off the bed as he loved her with his mouth. She couldn't move, couldn't do anything but feel the way he felt against her. She felt the tension fade away and the mounting pleasure begin to spiral out of control. Her legs were shaking as she climbed that ultimate peak to release. She let go of her resolve and fears and put her hands in his hair and let go.

He felt her release, and the way her legs were trembling made him ache for her more. He moved above her and watched her face as he moved to push inside her. She was tight, and it took more than one pushed to fully envelope himself within her. With a final push, he was exactly where he needed to be. He pushed her knees up and over his shoulders as his movements became more frantic, more demanding. Soon, he stood back from her, one hand holding each knee as he pounded into her relentlessly. He heard her moans, and knew she was sharing in the intensity. Her hips moved with his, and the explosion was powerful as he pushed into her one last time and release came.

They both lay there, trying to breathe and trying to make sense of what just happened. For Chloe, it was unlike anything she ever experienced. She looked up at him and he was smiling down at her. He leaned in and kissed her lightly before he stood up. She once again marveled at his chiseled body. He saw her glance and smiled at her. Hopefully she knew that he found her sexy and he enjoyed touching her. He made his way to the kitchen and Chloe quickly redressed. What had she done? She felt the blush rising up her face. He had seen her, all of her. No one ever had. She made her way into the bathroom and then followed him in the kitchen.

His phone rang and she turned to look at him and he frowned as he listened.

"Chloe, I have to go. I'm sorry, something came up."

"Sure it's fine go ahead." She felt the same fear from before, he would leave now.

"Chloe look at me." She did. "I will be back, I promise. " He kissed her quickly on the head and left.

To say he was worried was an understatement. The twenty minute drive took him 12. He pulled into his lot and stared up at the flaming mess. His penthouse was on fire and all he could do was watch. He found the house staff and was happy they were okay. The three of them watched as the fire department did their best.

The next few days Braden spent sifting through what had once been his home. His home hadn't been saved and very little else had either. He had to meet with the investigator today and then the adjuster. The police assumed this was an accident, but he wasn't as sure. He was staying at a nearby hotel, trying to hold it all together, but barely. He made sure the staff had rooms and that they were well taken care of. Most of his time was spent on the phone or on conference to various media networks and the racing team. He thought about Chloe, her smile and her sweetness. He missed her. Everything he put into proving he liked her the way she was vanished the night he left, and hadn't come back. He promised, and now she would never trust him again.

Chloe knew she was a fool. She spent that entire night waiting for him, as if she believed in his story, or that he would come back. She waited, and the joke was on her. Life had, inevitably gone back to normal. As a teacher, she threw herself back into the work of planning for the next school year. She found that by journaling a lot, she was able to keep her heart from hurting too much.

The reality was she cared about Braden and what he thought of her. The times they spent talking was a big part of that. He was a kind and sweet guy, despite his obvious fetish for big girls. It wasn't that he never came back that night. The fact was he had never come back at all, until yesterday. She hadn't actually seen him, just that his lights were on and music was playing inside. How he could just ignore her now was the brunt of the pain.

She wished for a moment that she had the strength to march over there and demand an answer, but it was better off left alone. She glanced at the clock and headed out to go grocery shopping. As she did, she heard the door open next door and she cringed. The last thing she wanted was a run in. She turned around and it was a woman, a very thin, very hot blonde woman. The blonde in question gave her a wave and she straightened her shoulders and left.

Braden had cancelled the rest of the afternoon and made the decision to try. He had to explain, and most importantly, he had to tell her the truth. He drove to her place and waited. He saw her car, he knew she was there, but for the first time since he was a child, he was scared. He was a nationally known bike racer and had been with more than a few women all over the world and this one woman had him questioning everything about himself. He felt the guilt like a punch in the stomach. Not just for leaving her like that, but for not telling her the truth about who he was. He finally got out of the car and went to the door.

She heard the knock and frantically made her way to the door. She found a solution to her financial woes and was moving in a roommate. To say the mess from what had once been storage was everywhere, would be putting it mildly. She climbed over the final boxes and pulled the door open. There he stood.

"What do you want Braden, I am really busy." She hoped the nonchalant way she talked to him would fool him.

"We need to talk Chloe, really talk." He sounded serious and she finally made eye contact. Still gorgeous, he looked rough. He looked tired and she knew something was wrong. She moved out of the way and he came inside.

He felt a sense of panic at the mess. "Are you moving?" He glanced around.

"No, I found a roommate. Nice guy, good job." She crossed her arms in front of her and waited. She would let him speak, but she wouldn't make it easy for him.

Braden felt a rush of anger. He would be damned if some "guy" was moving in here. "There are some things I need to tell you and explain. I need to know you will let me explain it all and then we will talk about this "guy" you think is moving in here."

He made his way to the living room and she followed. Her arms were crossed again and her eyes were flashing fire. Even now, he wanted her.

He turned the channel to ESPN and turned to look at her. "This is the best way I know how to explain."

She sat there stunned watching sports news, which she didn't even know existed. Some bike racer had a house that burned down and, wow, he was local. She suddenly felt sick. He was everywhere, pictures and stories and she knew. He turned it off.

"Oh my God Braden, are you ok?" She looked at him and touched his hand.

"I'm fine, my house is gone though. That's where I have been. That's why I didn't call."

"Why didn't you tell me you were famous? It would have made our fling that much more memorable for me." She gave him a half smile.

"Stop it Chloe, I don't look at you like that and I know you don't either. It's more than that and you damn well know it." She moved off the couch and towards the door. He caught her hand as she went by, standing up in the process. He kissed her forcefully, only letting go when they needed air. It was then he noticed her tears. He kissed her eyelids and wiped them away.

"Don't cry Chloe, please, I'm so sorry for everything." He pulled her into his arms and buried his head in her hair.

He kissed her face and then her mouth again. It started so simply, wanting to comfort each other, and soon they were lost in the moment. She pulled away from him and went up the stairs, and he followed. Once there, he took the lead, grabbing her hand and pulling her with him into the room. Their actions frantic now, they undressed each other. He turned her around to face away from him. She felt him unzip her dress and trail his fingers down her spine as the dress slipped to the floor. He reached around to cup her breasts, which overflowed in his hands. He pulled her back against him and she felt the hardness there.

"Don't ever question what you do to me Chloe, feel what you do."

She did just that, taking him into her hand and feeling the length of him. He pushed her over towards the bed and she climbed into it and he stopped her. She was half on and half off the bed when he moved behind her. He filled her suddenly and quickly, and she gasped at his entry. He moved his hand up to her hair, winding his fist in it and bracing himself as he plunged into her faster, and deeper. They moved together both seeking and searching for something. She was the first to reach her peak and she moaned out his name as she did so pushing him over the edge as well. He pulled her to him spooning behind her. She was his, and she always will be. Suddenly she stood.

"You should go Braden." She pulled her dress over her head and stood. He stood as well and she was once again reminded of how perfect he was.

"Chloe please."

"Braden this.... this was a mistake. You know it as well as I do."

"No, it's not a mistake, how can you even say that after what just happened?"

"We come from different worlds, Braden, you're... famous for God's sake and I am just some..."She trailed off. "You lied to me, Braden."

"I know, at first I just wanted you. I was driven by a need to be inside you, loving you. Then things changed."

"No, they didn't Braden... ...you should go... now."

He saw the firm set of her jaw and knew she was serious. He took one last look at her before he left. Chloe waited until she heard the front door shut and she locked it before crumbling to the floor and gave over to the tears.

Braden was not himself. His driving was awful and he couldn't connect with the course. He normally would love the flowing hills of Virginia, but he was officially not on a streak anymore. He angrily threw his helmet into the seat of the car and made his way to the crew. They all knew to avoid him when he was like this. Braden angry was a rare thing, but it usually had a quick turnaround. This time he was like this all day. He was angry, and worried. Chloe refused to respond to any messages he sent her and he missed her. She was so damn stubborn and it hurt that she didn't feel the same way.

Braden made his way into the hotel and caught a glimpse of himself in the mirror. He was dirty from the race, but he was changed now. He spent his entire adult life alone until this one woman came into it and now he was worried about someone else. He knew she had been struggling, in more ways than one. She shared her situation with him, told him her secrets, and he lied to her. He knew she was hurting, but couldn't she see how he felt? He frowned. How did he feel exactly? He got into the shower to wash away everything from the long day. He had to do something, and soon.

He met up with Mike for dinner that evening who put it all in perspective for him.

"You're in love with that chubby girl back home aren't you?"
Braden stood and towered over him.

"Don't ever say that about her again, do you understand me?"
"Whoa, whoa buddy calm down. I didn't mean anything negative about it. I am just telling you man, you got it bad. The whole damn crew is afraid of you the way you're tearing things up all the time. Not to mention you lost your streak, you need to see her and make it right. Either let her go or marry the girl."

Braden sat back in his chair and thought about what he said. Marry her? The thought gave him a start of panic, but the idea of coming home to her, all the time was one he could love. He ran his hand through his hair. He hoped she and Charile were okay, if only she would answer his damn calls. He suddenly had an idea, one that might make her call him after all. He pitched his idea to Mike, who chuckled and started to make the call.

Chloe was frustrated. The roommate was an ass and he left his things all over her house. More importantly, he was indifferent to Charlie. Treating him like a bug in his way all of the time. Last night was the final straw. He came home drunk and groped her, and she was finished with it. She took a deep breath before knocking on his door. She had to do it repeatedly before he finally yelled something and stumbled to open it.

"What Chloe?" He moaned as she pushed the door open wider.

"You have to move, Josh. I can't have this kind of environment for Charlie."

"You can't just kick me out, Chloe. I have rights. Besides, you like it when I touch you, don't even try to lie." He took a step towards her and grabbed her again. This time she pushed at him and scratched his face. He gave her one blow to the face and she staggered backwards. She rushed to the living room calling for Charlie and the two of them made their way out to her car.

Mrs. Anderson watched the little car pull away with a shake of her head. That was a bad man in there, she saw her holding her face when they left. She pulled out her phone to call Mikey and tell him the plan couldn't work now. After Mike hung up the phone, it took him a minute to turn around. He knew once he told Braden, he would lose it. There was nothing he could do but to tell him.

"Well, what did she say?" Braden was eager to hear Chloe was ok.

"Seems like she is gone man, I mean she had a couple bags and she and Charlie left."

"What the hell do you mean they left?"

"Sit down man I'll tell you everything."

Braden did, only because he knew he wouldn't get any information otherwise.

Twenty minutes later, Braden called the airline and booked a flight to Texas. The sonofabitch was going to pay and he would be the one to do it. Mike tagged along, mainly because he didn't want Braden to end up in jail. They took the direct flight and Braden was full of tension and ready to fight the entire time. Finally on the ground, they picked up a rental car and made their way into the city. He was practically out of the car before it even stopped. He made his way to her house and when the door opened, he let the first punch fly.

Mike glanced down at the man on the floor. The guy didn't even have a chance. Braden knocked him out with two hits. Braden made his way upstairs and checked to make sure she had yet to come back. He wasn't sure where she would go, she had a few friends, but no one she spoke about enough to give him any clear direction to head in. He walked back over to Mike's and sat in the chair by the window so he could watch and wait. He glanced up at Mike.

"Give me your phone."

"Why?"

"Just trust me, I'll give it right back."

He took the phone from Mike and sent a text to her from his number. He visibly relaxed when he got a response. It was wrong, but it had to work. She would be furious, but he would at least get to look at her and make sure she was ok.

Chloe was concerned. The message said that she needed to come home right away. She wasn't even sure who sent her the message, but she had to find out what was going on. She dropped Charlie off at a friend's house and made her way home quickly. She had so much to figure out and she was exhausted. She glanced at herself in the mirror. It had only been a number of hours, but her right eye was purple and bruised.

She couldn't go back in there. He was horrible. What had ever possessed her to let him move in in the first place? Money, always money. She wanted to keep Charlie in one place with his friends, something she never had, and this is what happened. She pulled into her parking lot and got out of the car. She would wait out here. She couldn't go in there alone ever again. It was then that the door next door opened and she saw him.

It was only a couple of months, but he was perfect. He took a few long strides to get to her and before she could say a word, he wrapped himself around her and picked her up. He literally picked her up. She heard him whisper her name and she closed her eyes against the emotional overflow she felt inside her. Why was he here? She pulled away and he stood back looking her over. When he looked at her face, he swore.

"That asshole." He started walking towards her place and she went after him.

"Braden wait." She went behind him and they made it to the door. She grabbed his arm. Suddenly there was another man there. He pulled Braden away.

"Calm down man." Braden turned towards her as the police pulled up out front.

"Oh no, Braden the police?" She walked towards the car again. She felt his hand on her arm.

> "Yes, the police Chloe. Look at your face and what he did to you." She tentatively touched her face with her fingertips. She saw the rage fill his face again and she touched him. "I'm fine Braden, really."

He watched her go speak to the police and he glanced at the front door as it slowly opened. Josh came staggering out and Mike once again grabbed Braden by the arm, preventing him from going to jail. The police made their way over to Josh and cuffed him. After they were gone, Braden turned to face her.

"We need to talk Chloe, now." He went inside and she soon followed, but not before Chloe saw the blond from before walking hand in hand with Mike. So she was never with Braden. Somehow that helped to make her feel a little better. At a wave from the two of them, she made her way inside where Braden was waiting.

"Braden, nothing has changed. I love that you came here to help me, I do, but we are still so different. Everything we do is..." She stopped as he kissed her. She closed her eyes, even if they couldn't be together, she could enjoy the way it felt when he kissed her, even just for another moment. She relaxed in his arms and he felt it. He pulled her even closer to him and ran his hands over her curves.

She was everything, and he wanted all of her. The kiss intensified and he undid the back of her dress pulling it to the floor. She was lost in him, his touch and felt the coolness of the air against her skin. She trusted him unlike she had ever trusted anyone else. He pulled her into the living room never stopping the kisses he trailed down her neck. When they made it there, she stopped him. She could be herself with him, for the moment. She walked around him and shed the rest of her clothes. She walked to the couch and laid back on it, fully unclothed and waiting. He watched her, his mouth hungry to touch her, but reveling in the way she was with him now.

She was no longer concerned about if he was attracted to her, or if he wanted her. She believed in him and how much he wanted to touch her. He finally moved towards her, gently moving his mouth down her chest, stopping to kiss and run his tongue over each crested peak. He buried his face in her breasts pulling on them and kissing every inch of them. She had her hands in his hair now pulling his head back up to kiss her deeply. He moved his hands along her curves and she arched up to meet them.

She moaned at the sensation and was aching for him with a need deep down. This is how he wanted her, how he needed her to be with him. He moved his fingers over her, working to a fevered state and he watched the expression on her face as she became more demanding of release. He wanted to give her more and he slid down, burying his face in her and tasting her.

He felt her hands in his hair as she grinded into him and finally he felt her reach that ultimate peak and he knew it was time. He raised above her, his excitement evident and she stood to touch him. Sliding her hands down his body over his chest and further until with a swift intake of breath, she held him in her hands. She slid to the floor, and when he saw her look up at him, it was almost too much. He pulled her up to him and kissed her deeply before pushing her to the couch again.

He mounted her swiftly, pushing into her depths. He reached the full hilt of himself and stopped. He wanted to just feel her surrounding him like this. He looked up at her face. She was flushed from her climax and eager for more, but he wanted to watch the expressions as he moved her. He moved slowly now stretching her to her limits and testing himself, his ability to prolong the inevitable.

He felt her hands on his chest as he looked down at her and he watched her curvy body move with his. He wanted her, always. He pulled out and slammed back into with a force that shook them both to the core. It had never been this good, this satisfying. The need was far too great and they both were aching to reach that final release. He moved faster now, steadily grinding into her and she was almost whimpering, and calling for him. He loved her like this, with abandon.

He increased his speed and was both grinding and pounding into her at the same time. It was good, too good. She called his name as her body moved on its own. She was no longer in charge of it and she felt the orgasm start low until it shuddered through her entire body, leaving her spent and breathless. Her explosion rocked him to the core and he couldn't hold back any longer. He slid his hands under her and lifted her off the bed slightly as he plunged into her again and again until he shared in her release. He buried himself inside her as far as he could. He wanted her to know he had given it all to her.

They lay there holding on to each other. Both afraid to speak, afraid to break the beauty of what they had shared. He knew she would run from him now, but he wouldn't let her. He was in love with her and he couldn't imagine life without her in it. She was the first to move, raising her head to look at him.

"Braden." She whispered and he gently kissed her lips. He held her that way, the two looking at each other waiting for the other to say something else. She was what he had been missing his entire life, she was family.

She raised up, suddenly self-conscious of her nakedness. He knew the person she was in the throes of passion was not who she was every day. It was a part of her she shared with only him, and he loved her all the more for it. He pulled her dress from the floor and helped her into it. He noticed she relaxed some and glanced at him sheepishly as she did it.

"Chloe, before you say anything, I need you to know something." He moved the strands of hair that had fallen into her face as she moved. She waited and looked up at him.

"I am in love with you." I know you don't know how this will work, but I know you have feelings for me too. I know you worry about everything, from yourself, to Charlie and money, and this house."

"Braden" she started, but he held up a hand to her...

"I'm not finished. The last few months have been the worst kind of hell for me. I found my mother dead on my living room floor when I was twelve, and aside from a loving couple who gave me a family for three years, I have been alone my whole life. I didn't even know what I was missing until you and Charlie. I love you. Chloe. I want you with me... you and Charlie. I have more money than I can ever spend and I want to share everything with you."

"Braden... I love you too." He relaxed with her words and pulled her closer to him. She was worried about life with Braden, what she never considered was how awful life would be without him. She smiled up at him and asked.

"Will you miss all the models and thin girls? Can I really satisfy you, Braden?

"Chloe, what we have is better than anything I have ever done in my whole life. You are sexy and gorgeous, and ALL I want is you." She smiled and a giggle escaped.

"What's so funny?"

"Charlie said you liked me even before any of this. Now I have to tell him he was right."

"I love you Chloe."

He kissed her again, and for the first time in her life, she believed it.

The Billionaire's Game

Sierra stared at her reflection and sighed heavily. Her hair, always tightly drawn up in a ponytail, gave the impression that she had a very angular face despite her chubbiness. She turned her head from side-to-side, looking at all of the planes that made up who she was. Her hair was a copper brown and her eyes blue. She had a smattering of freckles across her nose and cheeks that gave her a playful look. She had full lips that were always tinted as though she were drinking Kool-Aid, never forcing her to wear lipstick to give herself some more color.

Not that she ever wore make-up, really. As a waitress, she rarely had the time to care about things like make- up, or much else for that matter. She sat there contemplating what she could do to make herself pretty, or what she could do to improve her looks, or at the very least, make her more exotic or something.

She should have never agreed to stand in for Katie on a blind date. It's not so much that she was going to stand in for Katie on the date, it was that she had to actually pretend that she was Katie. It was just as much her own fault for saying yes, as it was Katie's for asking. She was always there for her, and this minor thing was no big deal, until now. She used her forefinger to push around the skin on her face, testing to see what she would look like if she had a face lift or something. That is until Katie herself came around the corner and gave her a short laugh.

"What the hell are you doing to your face, Sierra?" She said it with what remained of her scratchy voice.

"I'm looking at it, I wish I was more... I don't know, exotic or something." She continued to poke and prod.

"Why would you want to be exotic? You're beautiful the way you are." Katie made her way across the room. "I really appreciate this Sierra, it's a one-time thing, I told my mother I would go... and you know how she is." She rolled her eyes as she said it. Asking you to pretend you're me on a blind date is too much to ask, I know."

"I don't mind at all. I never get to go out, especially to a nice place like Giovanni's. Are you worried you will get found out somehow?" Sierra stopped long enough to glance at Katie, who was rifling through the make-up pile.

"No, Mom doesn't even know what he looks like or anything. She set this up for a friend of a friend or something. The guy's mother is desperate for him to find a nice girl and settle down because he's somewhat of a playboy. The only reason I agreed to this blind date was because I owe her for missing my cousin, Owen's wedding. I just wish I could have found a way out of it without dragging you through it."

Sierra glanced at Katie. "It's okay. This interview you have could really be a big break for you. You can't risk missing it by going on a blind date with a guy your mother fixed you up with. I understand, and like I said... free food. Who goes out on a Thursday night, though?" She gave her a smile.

Katie giggled. "So what are you wearing? Oh, and I'll do your make-up, maybe make you look more exotic!" They laughed together as they set out to getting Sierra ready for her date. They also had to figure out how to make the guy think that Sierra is really Katie.

An hour later, Sierra turned to take a long look at herself in the mirror. She was transfixed on her appearance. The Sierra she looked at everyday was gone, and in her place was a beautiful woman. Her hair, normally full of curls when left, down, had been straightened and now felt like silk on her shoulders. Her freckles were hidden and her eyes were the focal point of her face. Katie used her skills to give Sierra's eyes a dark and dusky look and she added some pink to her cheeks. Her dark lips only needed a hint of color, and she was definitely a different woman.

> "Are you gonna stand there and look at yourself all night or go get this silly date over with?" Katie was equally made up for her interview. The two of them stood side by side, staring at the mirror.

"I don't even look like... well me." Sierra giggled.

> "Well, tonight you're not you, you're me." Katie said simply as she picked up her bag to go. "Don't forget, meet him at the entrance at 7pm. He said he would have a red handkerchief in his jacket." Katie walked over to reassure Sierra once more. "I really do appreciate it girl." She gave her one last smile and she headed out. After Katie left, Sierra slipped on the tall black pumps Katie pushed on her to go with her outfit. She took a deep breath, and with a sigh, she left for the restaurant.

A.J. was frustrated. His latest business merger was in trouble, he was in desperate need of a woman and lastly, he had this blasted date tonight that he didn't want to go on. The day was dragging and he wanted to go. He flicked open the black book on the top of his desk and sighed. He had an unusual appetite and he needed something new, something exciting to help him calm down. This company... his company was everything to him. He built it from the ground up, and with it, he become an important figurehead in the community. The truth was they didn't really know him.

He had a dark side, one he kept hidden and he needed more. His appointments were short today. One merger meeting. Tomorrow morning he had one charity appearance for a donation he had made locally. He was always glad when the corporation could donate funds in the city where it was needed. It was almost a penance for the side of him that he couldn't control. He owed his mother his life and so, from time to time when she would request this of him, he would do it, to soothe her worried soul about the playboy reputation he had developed. He checked his reflection in the mirror and smiled to himself.

He was a playboy, and that suited him just fine. There were far too many women out there for him to have to settle for just one. He loved them all, and enjoyed his life exactly as it was. The unfortunate thing was that he was an only child and his mother was constantly on him about settling down and finding a nice girl to marry, to carry on the family name.

He gave his hair one last smoothing down before he put on his glasses and made his way to the waiting car. One of the perks of running a multi-million dollar company was the luxury of enjoying someone else driving you to and from.

He would be lying if he said he didn't get a thrill of impressing the ladies by having a driver when he pulled up to a new club in town. He liked to be impressive and his looks helped with that. He took care of himself, working out 5 days a week until he was toned. He had jet black hair, almost shaved on the sides and longer on top. His eyes were described as black by most and he always had a shadowed goatee. He was the epitome of tall, dark and handsome, and his evasive nature with women gave him an air of mystery.

He settled into the cool leather of the seats and leaned back to rest for a second. Hopefully, this night would go smoothly. The last time he went out with one of his mother's "girls" she bored him to tears until they made it back to his penthouse. There, she became a tigress and the sex was phenomenal. It was typical of his situation. More often than not, these girls would come in, hoping to find a husband and he would charm them right out of their clothes before they knew what happened.

This date would be the same, of that he was sure. He felt the car come to a stop and he made his way to the restaurant with ease. He gave the hot little hostess a smile and she started shuffling the papers in front of her as she blushed. It was almost too easy for him. What he wanted most was a challenge, something to work for, at least a little. He was led to a table in the corner, as requested , and he waited. As usual, he arrived early so that he could watch and decipher the woman his mother sent for him this time. It was almost like an animal stalking its prey. He leaned back some and waited with hooded lids.

Sierra took a deep breath before entering the restaurant. She was nervous that her date would find out that she really wasn't Katie. She knew she wasn't a mess since she was receiving appreciative looks from random men in the main entrance. She was led to a table, thanked the young lady who seated her, and turned to meet this month's "guy." She felt the blood in her veins warm up and her mouth go dry at the same time. He stood and extended a hand to her, helping her into her seat. She felt the faint presence of his fingers trace her back as he helped push her seat in. Before she choked on the water she was sipping, she decided to speak first.

"So, you must be A.J?" She took another sip.

Surprised by her forwardness, he raised an eyebrow. "I assume that makes you Katie. Yes, I am A.J. It's nice to meet you."

He had a voice that spilled out of his mouth like honey. She knew exactly why he was getting appreciative glances from the waitresses. He was almost too attractive. He had classic good looks with a mix of ruggedness which made it clear that he was no innocent poster boy, but rather a force to be reckoned with.

"It's very nice to meet you too. This is a nice restaurant. Do you come here often?" She was trying making small talk, and he knew she was nervous. He could tell by the way she sipped her water uncontrollably.

"No, I've only been here a handful of times, but it's very good, trust me." He gave her a dashing smile and Sierra knew in his simple off-handed comment that he was going to irritate her.

It wasn't his looks. The truth of the matter was that he was the most intensely gorgeous man she ever saw. That alone gave him some kind of arrogance that reached out of him. He was put together like a package. Every piece of him from head to toe was perfect. Part of her wanted to ruffle his hair and put him in sweats. He almost seemed too well put together. He was gorgeous, but his cookie cutter life made him unattractive to her, not to mention that he was far too sure of himself. She again sipped at her water as he watched her. It was almost unnerving.

"Do I have something on my face? You seem to either be lost in thought or overly concerned with what I'm doing." She said it simply and with a smile, and enjoyed the puzzled look that crossed his face.

"No, on the contrary. I was just looking at you, Katie." He delivered his words smoothly, and she had to stop her heart from racing. He gave her a smile and she felt her stomach lurch. She was as bad as the hostess. She rolled her eyes and glanced at the menu. With any luck, this would be over soon anyway.

He leaned back into the booth, watching her intently. She was so beautiful, it was almost painful. He enjoyed the banter they were having because she wasn't like most women. She had no idea how beautiful she was and that intrigued him even more. Usually the women he went out with were all superficial and very much aware of their beauty. They ordered their food and managed to make some small talk about nothing. He knew she was nervous and that gave him some sort of excitement. She moved without thought and enjoyed her food without counting calories. The entire scene was refreshing for him. She made an idle joke about the waiter, which he found amusing and they laughed about it.

"The decorating in here reminds me of a painting. I think art is beautiful." She gave him a half smile, less concerned about his good looks now that she was three glasses of wine into the date.

"Really? Maybe we should go to the art show that's traveling into town next week. I can get tickets fairly easy, actually." He gave her a smile and she felt the warm heat travel up from the pit of her stomach. He certainly had a way with words, and with women. She saw more than one lady go by to use the restroom and his eager attempts to greet each and every one of them. Playboy all the way.

He wasn't sure why he even asked her to the art show. She was definitely not his type, and not an easy conquest either. Perhaps it was the challenge that made him want her more. He gave her every look and effort that he possibly could, and she brushed him off at every turn. Maybe he wasn't her type, but whatever it was made him want her even more. Even now, as she hummed along to the ambient music in the restaurant, he wanted to kiss her full pouting mouth. He felt his pants tighten and he knew she would be his before they were through. Soon, dinner was over and they made their way outside. He walked her to her car and waited for her to look up at him.

"Well, I guess I'm gonna go." She gave a hiccup and a giggle, and he knew she wasn't going anywhere. He walked her over to the area where his driver was and after a moment of tapping on the roof, he safely tucked her into his car.

"Sorry, sweetheart, but you're not driving anywhere." He let his hand linger for a moment on her waist.

She was full of fire. "You can't kidnap me A.J. No way, Jose." She fell into a fit of giggles, then and he couldn't help but smile at her.

He felt the tension rise even more than before. As he clicked her in the seat belt, he was able to follow the line of her clinging dress up her hips and ending with a set of full breasts straining against the soft fabric, begging to be released. She looked up at him and he smiled at her. He wanted her. He knew it the second she looked up at him. There was something different and refreshing about her. Her hand trembled just slightly and he felt the heat rush through him. He let her go, watching as she straightened her clothes and looked at him.

Her heart was beating faster than usual and she wasn't sure why. He held her hand for just a second longer than necessary when he helped her in the car. He made his way around and slid into the seat beside her.

He looked up at her and leaned over closer. "I'm taking you home, you obviously cannot drive."

She felt a tremor go through her body as she felt his hot breath on her ear. He owned a really flashy car with a driver, it was one good sign, but even still, she was leery of getting into a car with someone she just met. The reality was, she didn't have much choice in the matter. She couldn't walk, let alone drive.

She gave him directions and soon enough they were at her apartment. He guided her up the stairs and soon she was inside. She felt her body come to life as he walked her inside. She watched him slide his eyes over the bed and then back to her.

"I hope you will be more careful Katie, perhaps not drink as much?" He reached out and took her hand in his.

His touch was sending little balls of fire through her veins and she knew this was dangerous ground. She felt his fingers moving along her wrist and he leaned towards her closer and closer still until she heard the front door open. Reality came crashing back in and she turned red as she glanced up at him. He stood slowly and moved towards her.

"Hey Sierra, I can't even begin to tell you how much stuff costs at the store now, I mean it's ridiculous." She stopped short at Sierra's door noticing the man inside. Sierra struggled to sit up some.

The blonde was much closer to his typical tastes. She had come bounding in full of sassiness.

Sierra gave her a look and Katie smiled. "So who is this?" She extended her perfectly manicured hand towards A.J. and he eagerly held it to his lips.

Sierra felt her face flaming as she explained the story, and how they came to end up here, now.

"Wait a second who is Sierra?" He gave them both a confused look.

"Me, I am... it's actually my middle name." Sierra gave Katie a sour look but he seemed to buy it.

"My name is Alayna, it is nice to meet you." She stifled a smile at Sierra. Alayna was actually Sierra's middle name. This was getting more complicated by the moment.

There was a moment of silence that passed between them before he took a step towards Sierra. He watched her for a moment as she struggled to stand, somehow trying to put herself together. She gave Katie an apologetic look.

"Well, I have to go back out, Katie, I'm glad your home safe, and A.J. thank you taking such good care of her. You two have a good evening." She winked at an angry Sierra before leaving the apartment.

He gave Alayna a wave and once she was gone, he turned to look at her. She wasn't sure what to do or feel. The alcohol in her system was more than she should have taken in and it had impaired her judgement. It didn't matter what she wanted really as he made his way over to her and leaned in close before his mouth made its descent on hers. He pulled her towards him and explored her mouth at length. He was radiating heat and she met his kiss with equal intensity. They moved together with him pushing her back into the couch and holding her arms above her head with one arm. He ran his hands under the hem of her dress and up along her thigh, she wanted him to touch her, but yet she didn't. He found the laced edge of her panties and she froze, finally coming to her senses. She was anticipating his touch when her phone rang, shattering the moment. What the hell, she inwardly cursed herself?

He stood now, facing her and looking down at her. He wasn't upset, but merely amused. He wanted her, eventually, but never like this. He stood once more and made his way to the door. Leaving her with an aching need she felt deep down and nothing to cure it. She glanced down at her clothes and straightened them quickly. What was wrong with her anyway? She always had control over her actions, but today she most definitely was not in control. What he must think of her, meeting him on a blind date and then within an hour letting him touch her like that.

"I'll pick you up next Friday at 8pm Katie, be ready, I can be impatient." He rebuttoned his jacket and smoothed his hair before dropping a quick peck on her forehead and leaving her stunned.

"What was he even talking about anyway?" she whispered to herself once he had left.

She hung her head in her hands and sighed. She had very strict rules about sex, and dating and right now she was breaking every one of them. She allowed herself a moment to try and recover, but she had been changed for good. Whatever she did, she would need to stay away from A.J.

The next week passed by and she did her best to stay calm and not think about him. Katie was making it nearly impossible with her line of questioning that seemed endless.

"Oh wow so you kissed him, that's it? Honey, he is gorgeous, I should have totally went on that date." She laughed at her own joke but seemingly aware of Sierra's unhappiness.

"Yes, and it was stupid because he is an ass, totally shallow and he thinks he is some gift put here for women to look at." She rolled her eyes. "Not to mention, he kissed that night's version of me, not the real me." She threw her bag into the window of the car.

"Maybe he is a playboy, and shallow and whatever, but the truth of the matter is he liked you Sierra, and when was the last time you went out and had any fun anyway? It's good for you, go enjoy it." She made her way to her car. "Byeee." She gave a wave.

"Whatever, be quiet Katie." She said it with a laugh as she settled into her car. It was then she noticed the note that was under the wiper. She moved to retrieve it.

That was only the beginning, I want you

She felt her body come to life with the excitement of the words. He certainly had no problem sharing what he wanted, but she had decided to not let it go any further than it already had. She had very strict guidelines about how she lived her life. She had been reckless and let the fantasy take over yesterday. It had been the make-up, the dress and the stupid wine. Nothing more. She wouldn't let it happen a second time. She needed to focus on the important things in life like her family, and taking care of herself. She made her way towards the town where she had grown up. She was off this morning and was going to see her little brother off to his first day of school. She loved the small town charm that made up the community where she used to live. It was hard to imagine that just two towns over the city was overfilled with people and congestion. It was good to sometimes come home and put things into perspective. She only hoped to not run into A.J., ever. He had wanted that woman from dinner, not the one getting ready to visit her family in a sundress and flip flops. The fantasy was something she couldn't give him, or anyone for that matter. All she had to do was get refocused.

She saw her little brother in the front yard with their father and she got out of the car just in time to hop into the SUV that would take the four of them to the school. He was excited, and scared, she could tell by the way he was fidgety but not talking much. Having a child after so many years since Sierra had been a struggle for her parents, but they loved Jacob more than anything in the world. He had been a miracle child for them really, and completely unexpected. She had been 16 when he was born and the shock had just subsided about having a new toddler running around when he was getting ready to go to school. Even harder was the fact that her brother needed medication for his condition. When he was five he had been diagnosed with myeloid leukemia. The medication alone had cost her father their savings. She knew she needed to do something to help, but she wasn't sure what. She looked down at her brother and put her hand on his knee and he moved his to hers smiling, then after a second she tapped his nose and he would tap hers back. Finally, she stuck out her tongue and he followed suit. He relaxed as she tickled him in the back seat.

The brick building was spread out ranch style and had two wings. It was a beautiful undertaking and after years it was finally ready. She walked hand in hand with Jacob, her father ahead of them. He really was a good boy. They watched as the announcer made a speech about the importance of family. It was then that she froze. She heard his voice before she even looked down towards the podium. He was dressed impeccably as he had been yesterday. He was far away enough that he did see her but she watched him as he shared the importance of meeting educational goals. That was where she had recognized his name. Trager Enterprises was the largest business in the area and often would give money to local causes. It was his money that made this building possible. The old school had been falling apart and now, apparently with his help, they had a new one, one that had a special wing for children with illness like Jacob. She felt her heart soften a little towards him. This knowledge would only make it that much harder to stay away from him.

She walked with Jacob and her father to his class. She felt the sense of loss once he was inside for them both. She only wished her mother could have been there to see him go inside. Just two years ago, she was killed in a tragic car accident that left her and her father with Jacob. They did the best they could and now he was getting older. Her father headed back to the car and she waited a few seconds longer wanting to remember this moment for her mother. She turned to leave and there he was, leaning against the wall watching her again.

"Hello Katie." He enunciated her name strangely and gave her a stormy look.

"Mr. Trager hello... again. My brother is a student here now. This is a great thing you did." She knew she was rambling and gave him one final look. "It was nice to see you again." As she walked by him, he grabbed her arm pulling her towards him.

He kissed her lightly and let her go, it was almost a tease, but enough to remind her that he was in control. She started walking as soon as she was free and she tried to calm her racing heart as she did it. She saw his dark smile as he turned to leave. He was the most arrogant person she had ever met that she knew. She touched her fingertips to her lips still tingling from his latest onslaught. How was it he managed to show up places when she was there?

She headed to lunch with her father before heading back into town. They had just sat down when suddenly he was there. She almost choked on her water.

"Sierra, Mr. Trager is having lunch with us. It seems we he knows you and in mentioning lunch I asked him to join us." She smiled weakly and looked up to catch his eye. It was as if he were looking right through her.

"How nice." It was all she could manage to squeak out.

"Sierra, are you okay, you looked pale." Her father seemed genuinely concerned.

"Yes, you look as though something shocked you or something of that nature." He interjected with the same smile that drove her crazy.

"I'm fine, just some pesky bugs in the hall before that's all." She saw his smile again but he said nothing.

Lunch was an interesting time. He spoke and laughed with her father as if there was nothing underlying between them. He asked her to show him the gardens at the café and at her father's insistence she did.

"You look beautiful today Miss Ford." He glanced over at her as they walked.

"Thank you Mr. Trager." She refused to look at him.

"So, when were you going to tell me that you are not Katie?" He never broke stride.

"How did you find out?" She crossed her arms over the front of her dress as they walked.

"Does that really matter? The reality is you lied, I don't do well with liars." He said it stiffly. She felt the anger start to rise deep down.

"Oh really, well, it's a good thing it was only one date." She flashed her eyes at him and saw him do his best to hide a smile.

"Have I mentioned how badly I want you?" she tripped lightly and he caught her arm.

"Really? Why would you say something like that to me?" She stopped to look at him.

"It's simply the truth, if I want something I find it much easier to get if I simply make it clear." He took a step towards her and she started walking again as he chuckled.

"You're safe for now, Miss Ford. One day soon I won't keep that promise." She glanced at him, but he continued to look at the pond beside them.

"Your almost a different person today Sierra, more free and happy perhaps."

"I am in my own clothes, and I'm at home. I supposed I am free that way." He stopped her and looked down into her face.

"I like you better this way." There was a long moment between them and she broke free and made her way up the path. He chuckled.

"Tell me about your brother."

There was something in the way he said it that made her feel close to him. He seemed genuinely interested and she shared her story with him. Her brother had been diagnosed with a form of leukemia. He listened and interjected when necessary. He was almost a different person in this environment. She found him easy to talk to and strangely, she felt safe with him. He spoke about some of the new directions the company was going in and she listened, interested in the way business is managed. She gave him some input and he arched an eyebrow at her point of view.

She was happy she had at least shown more to her character than the way she behaved around him before. Right before they made their way back to the café he stopped and pushed her into the overhang kissing her again, quickly but deep and hard. He stopped and pulled away slightly before he backed away completely. They made their way back to the table where her father sat and Trager jumped right back into the conversation as if it were nothing. They parted ways and she rode back with her father to get her car.

"That Mr. Trager is a nice guy, Sierra." She looked over and he gave her a wink.

"He is an ass dad, plain and simple." She crossed her arms in the car and he smiled at her but didn't say another word.

She missed home when she wasn't there, but she loved the city more. She said her goodbyes to her father and headed back to the apartment. She pulled her car into the lot adjacent to her apartment building and her phone started ringing. She assumed it was A.J. and ignored it since her hands were full. The second time it went off after she had been inside for a few minutes she checked it. It was work, with a sigh, she called Harry back at the diner.

"Sure Harry, I'll be there just as soon as I can ok?" With a sigh she pulled her hair back into a bun and threw on her uniform. Hopefully since it was a Friday she would make decent tips.

The night seemed to drag on as she made her usual rounds. Despite her effort to not think about him, he was there and present in her mind. Maybe Katie was right, maybe she needed to get out more, and have fun. Things had been a mess since Jake and she couldn't seem to move past it. There was some level of trust she couldn't seem to give too freely to anyone. She was tired and she was unhappy. Sure, she had great friends, but she was living paycheck to paycheck and she needed to get things together. Her classes here and there were certainly not helping to propel her career in any way. She had big plans once upon a time and now she was just surviving. She felt someone touch her apron and glanced back to see another staggering drunk trying to touch her rear. She pulled the apron away and made her way to the counter. She let her head hang in her hands for a second refusing to give in to the stress, she was only 26 she still had time to get it together. Finally, the night came to a close and she headed home lost in deep thought about her future.

The next morning was there too quickly and she rolled over with a sigh. Today would be busy. The only day the she could actually clean the apartment and get it together. They both worked and went to school all week and rarely got anything done. She knew that Katie was still sleeping. She shuffled her way to the kitchen lost in thought once more about her brother. His prognosis, if medicated was good, but she worried about him. She looked around and jumped in full force. She would be lying if she said she didn't think about him. It was strange, someone making her feel things now. She had assumed that was all behind her. She wanted desperately to be like Katie. To find love and happiness, but none of it was for her. She needed to focus on what was important.

A.J. was having a similar morning. He was killing himself waiting to find a woman. Usually he could go out and find any number of them to bring home, but now he was stuck. He told himself it had nothing to do with her, but he wasn't so sure. Ever since their kiss at the school opening he couldn't get her out of his head. This was the first day in a long time he woke up unsatisfied from the night before. He always had someone, but she had robbed him of it. He was completely focused on winning her over. He wanted her even now, in his bed. He gritted his teeth and made his way to the shower. Sometimes it helped, sometimes not. Soon, however, she would be his even if only for one night.

The rest of the morning flew by and Sierra looked around enjoying her clean apartment. There was a sense of pride in that and she liked order. She never would be considered spontaneous on any level. She slumped down in the chair and threw the rag in she had in the waiting basket. Soon Katie would be gone, moving for her new job, and she would either have to find a way to make the payments on this place herself, or move home. She liked the simplicity of the apartment, but she was doubtful there was any way she could make it on her own. For now she would enjoy it.

He knew she would be mad. Furious more likely. She wanted him as much as he wanted her, but she was determined to fight him. She was always leery of him, part of him liked it that way, and he enjoyed the banter they seemed to find themselves in every time they spoke. She was smart and quick, he knew that by talking to her, but something kept her from giving in to him and he wanted to know what it was. He wanted her and he rarely was ever turned down. She was fighting him and the chase had begun. When she was here, which he was sure would be within the hour, he had every intention of claiming her body once and for all. The morning seemed to go on forever as he anticipated the way she would feel beneath him. He wanted to control her every move and the thought flooded him with fire. Soon, he thought to himself, soon.

He heard the first stirrings of activity in the lobby. He smiled and leaned back in his chair waiting and anticipating how she would look when she was angry. He spun around as his assistant opened his door.

Mr. Trager someone, a young lady is here to see you. "She glanced behind her quickly. "She said you were expecting her."

"I am, please let her in." He sat up and made every effort to look busy as she stormed into the room.

As soon as he heard the click of the door, he looked up at her and it hit him like a punch to the gut. She was more beautiful at this very moment than she had been yet. Her hair was a swirling mass of reds and browns and flowed down her back freely. He could almost feel his fingers itch to run through it. Her arms were crossed and her body was fitted into a dress that hugged her every curve and angle.

"What the hell were you thinking towing my car?" She continued to tap her foot as she waved a sheet of paper at him. "I had to take a cab to get here and even that took forever. I can't afford to take a cab all the way across town, Trager." She huffed and exhaled slowly and he noticed the pink hue of her cheeks,

"I'm sorry Sierra, I wanted you to come see me, and I knew this was one way to make it happen." He leaned back and smiled.

"You are so smug sometimes, A.J., you just assume the world is here to give you whatever you want aren't you?" She was practically yelling and he wanted to somehow bottle up all the fire she carried and make love to her for hours.

"Sometimes, yes. I like getting what I want and right now I want you." He said it simply enough, but there was much more to the statement.

"You don't even know me, Trager." She sighed.

It was the truth and it had never been clearer to her than right now. He had no idea of what was on her plate, or in her world for that matter.

She was already stretched too thin and it wouldn't take much to push her over the edge. Her Monday started out badly, her car was towed, and she'd spent hours on the phone looking for various agencies to help fund Jacobs's medication. Money was running out and she needed a solution fast. Her father called her to discuss the house and he decided to take out a loan against it. It was the only thing of value he had left that he'd shared with her mother. With the growing figures for Jacobs's medication, it was clear he had no choice. Then after going outside and seeing that her car was missing, she stomped off in search for it, only to find it had been a ruse to get her here.

"I want you in my arms Sierra. I have wanted to touch you since that night when I watched you walk into the restaurant."

"I don't know how you do it, Trager, but for me, I am not interested in becoming some notch on your headboard."

"I don't have a headboard, Sierra, but you will see soon enough." His arrogance was stifling, but she couldn't stop the warmth that spread through her body. "I know you want the very same thing from me but you won't let yourself go. I am not asking for marriage or family, I just want you, plain and simple."

He was almost too much to look at. He was impeccably dressed as always. He delivered his point clearly and effectively and she knew what he said was true. She wasn't too old yet to want to be touched by someone, and held by someone. The obvious problem was that she wasn't that type of girl.

"Shut the door, Sierra." She did as he told her, and as she started to walk towards him, he added "lock it."

With a gulp she did as she was told. There was an underlying current in the air and she could tell he was playing with her, like a cat and mouse game. She wouldn't be bossed around by his arrogance and she wanted him to know it. The entire situation was out of hand and she let it go too far that day in her apartment. She took responsibility for drinking the wine that got her into this mess.

"Mr. Trager, I think I need to apologize. I think I may have given you the wrong impression about me. I am not the kind of girl who just lets strange men touch her... well you know what I mean. I can't let this... attraction between us continue." She fumbled the words out. "To say that my life is complicated right now would be a very sincere understatement."

They sounded less harsh than she intended, but she finally got them out. He turned slowly towards her and he had a sinister look about him. He wasn't frowning, or smiling, but it was as if he was stuck between both. He moved towards her like a cat chasing its prey and she backed up against his desk as he moved over her. He was slow at first. He simply ran his finger across her neck relishing at her quick intake of breath. He looked at her as he traced his finger across her chest and across the tops of her breasts. She couldn't breathe, it was if she had never said a word. He kissed the tops of each mound lightly before he undid her hair, letting it cascade around her like a fiery blanket. He put his hands in it and pulled her hard against him, crushing his mouth to hers. She was lost. The feel of his mouth, grinding into hers was a welcome one. She tried to put up a defense against him and failed. He turned her around and she felt him lean into her as he whispered into her ear.

"Sierra, I have been very clear about the fact that I want you. I want you to know that before anything else happens. I want you to know without any doubt that it's going to happen." She gasped as he pushed against her and she could feel the length of him against her.

"You have to let go, let yourself feel all of the things I want to show you." He kissed her mouth lightly. "If you want to say no I will, but understand if you do, I may not try again."

She nodded yes to him as the rest of her defense slipped away. He was very matter-of-fact about things and she loved it. She felt him unzip her dress and trail his fingers down her spine as the dress slipped to the floor. She was aware of every nerve ending in her body as his hands reached around and touched her.

"Don't move." It was all he told her before he began his descent.

Even in slow motion Sierra couldn't stop the kiss, she welcomed it more than she should have and she shivered as she felt his other hand under the other side of her head. He raised back only once searching her face and seeing no resistance, he kissed her once more. This time deeper, longer and more demanding. She felt him cup the back of her head to tilt her towards him as the kiss intensified.

She didn't want to fight anymore, couldn't fight anymore. She stood and with one zip she let her dress drop to the floor leaving him speechless. She made her way over to him and he felt her tentatively put her mouth on his. This kind of forwardness was completely out of her comfort zone and he knew it.

"How long has it been Sierra?" Her eyes flew open to look at him.

"Four years." She whispered it to him and it almost pushed him over the edge.

She let him love her in a way she had never known. Most of it was undoubtedly because of his experience as a lover. There was a sense of panic she'd felt when he told her there may not be another chance. She wanted to feel good, feel better. Her life was a mix of stress and planning and all she wanted was to feel something else. His skin on hers was like fire and ice and she let go, of her fears, of her stress of everything and he loved her completely. She met his every move and every action and she knew she was giving him as much as he gave her.

A.J. was moved by what had happened between them. He had certainly been with many women, but nothing had ever been as moving as what they had shared. She had always been distant and scared and yet something switched and she gave instead herself to him with everything in her power. She wasn't shy or meek, she was eager and demanding and he enjoyed pushing her to her limits. Yet, as good as it was, she was holding back something he couldn't quite put his finger on. She lay cupped in front of him and he could sense she was exhausted and simply didn't want to move. It wasn't usually his style, cuddling, but for her he would make an exception. There was a sense of sadness about her he wanted to fix, despite the warning bells in his head. He traced his finger up and down the length of her arm as she dozed slightly. No, this wasn't his usual situation on any level at all. It happened almost simultaneously, the two of them remembering where they were. Sierra jumped up to start gathering her clothes. To be honest, the fact that they were in his office was mortifying and she was blushing the entire time. Along the way that fact had slipped her mind, until now.

"Sierra... Sierra calm down it's fine." He smiled at her as she continued to slip back into her clothes and he was able to be a bystander and admire the curve of her hip and the softness of her skin as the light hit it.

"No A.J. it's not alright. This is not me, I mean not really me." She was frantic in her actions and after he redressed, he stilled her arms and helped her to breath. He sensed a panic in her, something deep down.

"Do you want to talk about it Sierra?" he brushed her hair back from her face as he cupped her chin lovingly.

"No, no I'm fine, I'm sorry. I have to go." She gave him one last look and headed out of the office in a hurry. Something was wrong and he wanted to know what it was.

She took the few strides to reach her building and once inside her room, she collapsed against the door. What was she thinking? No matter what she did, she somehow managed to make the situation worse. She shook her head to clear her thoughts of him and what had happened, and called home. Her father answered and they took some time to discuss the home loan further. He sounded tired and she worried about him. She also spoke with Jacob about school. He was excited about the teacher and his class. She missed his little face all the time. She listened to her father and told him about work and Katie, she failed to mention Trager. They chatted for a while discussing the options she had once Katie was gone. Her last day at work was yesterday and she would be another week packing and getting things ready before leaving. Finally, they hung up and she carefully stood to walk into the kitchen. She blushed, remembering. Even now, she was sore from what he put her through. She had to remind herself that it could never happen again. She took a drink of water and settled into the armchair in the living room. Katie had been gone for hours, having met a friend in town. For the next few hours she had the place to herself and she planned to use them wisely. She started running a bath, touching the hot water with her fingertips. She was soaking for ten minutes before she heard a loud thump on the front door. She sat up quickly and wrapped herself in a robe. She felt her heart beating fast as she made her way to the front door. She checked the eye hole and saw no one. She froze when she saw the shadow of someone in the hall.

She opened the door to look. He stood back looking at her.

"Sierra, hey look don't shut the door." He rushed towards her block it with his arm.

She folded her arms. "What do you want Brandon, why are you here and

Furthermore, how did you know I was here?" He pushed the door slightly and came inside.

She took a step back, this was part of the problem between them. He scared her. With A.J., she knew he wouldn't hurt her. With Brandon, it made her worry, about her safety.

He reached out to her. "Sierra, I miss you so much, if you would just let me show you." He took a step towards her and she moved out of his reach, grabbing the vase on the table and moving away.

"Brandon, please. You know it's done with us you can't do this. I need you to go." She moved towards the door and he grabbed her arm. She knew there would be bruises tomorrow. It was then that the front door opened and Katie came through it, followed by someone she had never met.

It was obvious they had walked into something dicey and the man with Katie spoke up first. "Is there a problem here?"

Katie made her way over to Sierra hugging her as she walked her towards the kitchen.

"No man, not a thing, I was just going. Sierra, I'll be back." Brandon said as he left and he shut the door.

Sierra was visibly shaken, she had never expected him to follow her here. She had thought to leave him behind and start over.
"Thanks, I appreciate the help." She glanced over at Katie.

"Sierra this is Marcus, a good friend of mine." She gave Marcus a huge smile and Sierra shook his hand.

"No wonder you sent me on that crazy date." She gave them both a half smile, still reeling from Brandon's visit. "Really though, thanks for your help. She excused herself to go think.

She made her way to her room. She had no choice, she would have to go home now, and at least with her father around, she felt safe. She supposed she could call the police, but she wasn't sure much would come of it. Instead, she focused on her assignment for the class she was taking online. Monday, she would give a notice at the diner.

Brandon didn't bother her anymore the rest of the week. Two of her tires were slashed on Friday morning and she was beginning to wonder if it was Brandon all along. She had Katie drop her off at the diner. She would normally be happy and carefree, but now she was depressed and wasn't sure how to get out of the way she felt. More than that, she was scared and worried about where she was headed. The day went by quickly and she made her way home on the bus, hoping to just get there safely. She jumped when her phone rang and she checked the number and relaxed. It wasn't Brandon.

"Hello A.J., how are you?"

"I'm doing well, I was hoping maybe we could talk, before our date tonight."

She frowned, thinking, she had not only forgotten about the date, some part of her assumed he had been joking anyway. Given the last time they had seen each other she almost figured she wouldn't hear from him again.

"About that A.J., I'm not sure if I can. Some things have come up I need to take care of. Besides, I don't have a car."

"Even better, I'll send you one, are you at home?"

"Yes, but..."

"Give me thirty minutes." He cut her off mid-sentence and then hung up abruptly.

The truth of the matter was that she wasn't sure if she could handle seeing him right now. With the possibility of Brandon lurking about, she was consumed with worry. A.J. probably never had these kinds of issues. On top of her own problems, she was concerned about her father and Jacob. Based on her calculations, even with taking out a loan on the house, he would need more money down the road. What would they do then? She considered A.J., not for the first time either. If she could somehow get him to fall for her then she would have the financial freedom to help Jacob, but it was completely out of character for her to do something like that. Even still, the idea burned in the back of her mind. She couldn't admit to herself even now, that she may want to get him to fall for her because she just wanted to be with him, it was ridiculous to even think it. He was a known playboy and he would never settle for her no matter what she wanted, on the surface or deep down.

True to his word a car arrived to pick her up. She made the attempt to put on something nice. She had on a black dress and heels and her hair was spun up on top of her head. She applied her make–up, much as Katie had done before, but just not as much. She sat back to see how she looked and once again the person staring back was a stranger. She would at least try to test the waters, to see if he felt anything for her. They had only known each other a short time, but there was something there and they both knew it. She watched the buildings fly by, lost in her own thoughts. Nothing made sense anymore. A.J. Trager had her head spinning and it wouldn't allow for her to focus on what was important. She would test the waters, so to speak, to see what he said and felt about her. She had zero powers of seduction up her sleeve, but she would try, for Jacob. The car pulled up to his building and she made her way inside and up to his floor. Since he towed her car, she knew exactly where to find him now, he had been nice enough to send her money back to her for the car and the tow with a courier, but it was still about the principle. She smiled at his assistant, a blonde who was gorgeous, and couldn't help but wonder if he slept with her too.

She heard his voice welcome her in and she took a deep breath and went inside. He looked up from the papers on his desk and sat back in his chair. He was all business-like and the air that surrounded him seemed to come to life. She glanced at the desk and gulped. Just a few days ago, she was laid out in that very spot. She felt the redness rush to her cheeks.

A.J. looked her over. He usually had a firm handle on his behavior, but he struggled with not finding her since she had last been here. Not even 30 minutes after she left during her last visit, he felt himself wanting her again. She was under his skin and he was trying to figure out how to handle it. Something was very different today, she was as pale as a ghost and almost lifeless despite her efforts to seem calm and carefree. He tried to push down the need to fix whatever was bothering her. Instead he stood and walked towards her.

She saw him coming and despite her fears she felt the fire almost immediately. He made her come to life and feel safe all at the same time. He stopped and leaned back on the desk.

"Come here, Sierra." She obeyed him. He lifted his hand up to her pale face and traced the line of her jaw with his forefinger. "Did you think about me about what we did?" She nodded her head yes and her eyes met his. He frowned because she was not completely here with him, not now.

"What's wrong Sierra?"

"Nothing, why do you ask." She gave him a warm smile and reached up to run her fingers over his sports coat.

He frowned. She was doing her best to appear seductive, but her actions didn't match her appearance. There was something going on but she was hiding it from him, toying with him. There was a loud bang from the outer office and she practically jumped into his arms. She buried her head in his chest and instinctively he wrapped his arms around her.

His door opened to reveal his assistant. "Sorry about the commotion, Mr. Trager. The Adams kids were here and they decided to play a prank on Dad. They have since left and Mr. Adams apologized for their behavior." She gave him a quick glance and took in the scene of him holding that nice girl whose car he had towed.

"Thank you for letting us know." He gave her a smile and once the door was shut, he addressed the woman who was wrapped around him.

"Okay, Sierra, what's going on, what's wrong?" She pulled away from him.

"Nothing is wrong, A.J... I just had a rough night and I apologize for my behavior. I didn't mean to embarrass you like that." She sniffed and he frowned at her.

"No, I'm not letting this go Sierra, I want to know why you are trembling like that, and now!" He was demanding and loud and she worried someone would hear them outside of the doors.

"I may as well tell you, there has been a situation that has come up and I will be moving in a week or so. I guess I'm just nervous or stressed, that's all." She trembled slightly as he took her hand in his and turned it over, lightly tracing the palm with his thumb.

He pulled her to him and she welcomed the arms that wrapped around her, holding her. She knew then she could never seduce him. Hell, she wasn't even able to have a conversation with him without falling apart. She felt his hands rubbing her back and she closed her eyes, enjoying the way his hands felt. He moved them now, running them down the length of her and she trembled now, not from fear, but of what she knew his hands would do to her if she didn't stop them now. She tried to pull away from him, but he held her there and she looked up at him.

"Didn't you like what I did the other day to you, Sierra?" He pulled her arm up and nibbled his way up the underside of her forearm. "Answer me, Sierra."

"Yes." She whispered the words as her body reacted to him. She had all the strength in the world when he wasn't in front of her. When he was she was lost to him.

"Is your family in trouble?" He continued up her arm having moved around to the top of her shoulder now.

"No, well yes, but no." She frowned, unsure how to answer him.

"Then you can't leave me, I'm not done with you yet." He pulled her face to his and kissed her roughly, needing to feel the softness of her full red lips beneath his.

She knew she had no choice, she had to go, but right now she was here, with him... safe. He pulled back and without thought she pulled his head back down to hers. Without warning, he stopped and backed away from her. She trembled, watching his face and took a step back.

"I have to touch you Sierra, do you understand? I have thought of nothing else." He moved back towards her and pulled her towards him by the arm. She whimpered and he let her go. He may be passionate, but he would never hurt her. He gently pulled the arm out of the sleeve she was wearing, despite her protests and looked at the black and purple bruise forming on her arm. He felt the rage well up inside him and knew he wanted someone to hurt for this.

"Who did this to you, Sierra?" She looked at the floor and shoved her arm back in her sleeve to go. He grabbed her chin, forcing her to look at him. "Who?"

She knew he wouldn't give in until she answered him. "He is an ex, I moved because of him and he found me." She watched the play of emotions on his face as he stood. "Don't move Sierra, I mean it." He walked over to the window and she stood rooted to the spot. He was on the phone talking to someone and when he was through he made his way back over to her.

"My driver is on his way here, you are to let him take you to my place where I know you will be safe and wait for me until later."

"Mr. Trager, that's not necessary, this is not your problem, it's mine." She stood to go, but felt him move between her and the door.

"Sierra, I am not arguing with you about this? Where is your car I'll have it brought to your house."

"You sent a car for me, remember? Someone slashed my tires." She said it dryly and he swore under his breath. There was a knock on the door and he simply said "Open."

He spoke to his driver for a moment before he walked over to her. He was almost gentle in the way he led her to the door. "I will see you there later." He stopped and turned her around to face him. "Tell me you will be there Sierra, I don't have time to worry about you all afternoon."

She knew he was serious and she would do as she asked. "Yes, I'll be there A.J..." As the driver left the room, he pulled her into a kiss. "I'll be there soon."

"Where am I going, A.J.?" she asked it simply but he knew she needed to feel safe.

"To my place, you will be safe there." At her hesitation he added. "Just do this... for me." She looked up at him and knew he was sincere, she nodded her head yes. He kissed the top of her head as she left.

She made her way down the elevator and to the waiting car. She planned to seduce him, to help her family. Somewhere along the way she simply planned to tell him she was leaving. As usual, he took over the conversation and made the decisions for her. She visibly relaxed in the seat. She needed to feel safe for a little while anyway. She knew she would be gone in a few hours, but for right now she would be at his house, where her ex can't find her.

Nothing prepared her for the penthouse where he lived. It was obvious to her that he had refined and elegant tastes in everything. From the marbled counters, to the floor to ceiling windows. She felt out of place here, like a dirty stray puppy or something. The driver, she found out on her way here, had been working for Trager for two years and was close to him. He led her to the main room where she could relax. Twenty minutes later he returned with a box in hand.

"What's this?" She took the box and lifted the lid slightly. Once she saw the lace, she closed it immediately.

"Mr. Trager said to make sure you were fed and had something to wear. He also ordered food for dinner and it will be here before he arrives.

"You have full use of the house, Miss Ford." He tipped his hat and left her. She spun around the room and set about exploring. She found a huge bedroom with a canopied bed, and adjacent to it was a marbled bathroom. To say it was elegant was an understatement. She filled the large oval bathtub and decided to slip in and try to enjoy it. She redressed in her work clothes. The "outfit" he gave her was a sexy lacy thing, barely there. It was a dark blue color and he tucked a note inside that read:

I will be there at 6, wear this... and your hair down.

She had to smile, he was so demanding and yet it suited him. She thought about the next steps for her and where she would go from here. It all came back to the same conclusion. She had no choice but to go home. She lifted her arms to brush out her hair with her fingers and winced in pain, once again reminded of Brandon, and his declaration that he would be back. She heard the door and felt the same fear creep in and then she remembered the food. She checked, and opened the door to a lovely young woman with an arm load of boxes. She put them all in the warming oven and looked at the clock. It was 5:45. She decided she would wear it, for him. He was sweet enough to let her come here to feel safe. It was the least she could do. She tried to deny it had anything to do with the fact that they would be alone in his house. She also had thrown the idea of seducing him out the window. For now, she just wanted to erase the past couple of days and feel something good. She changed her clothes and waited.

He came home quietly, barely a sound. Something that didn't shock her. He moved into the room and dropped his things as he took long strides to get to the bedroom. He froze when he saw her there. Slowly he undid his tie and started undressing.

"Come here Sierra, help me." She did as he asked, watching his face as she stripped him of his clothes. His skin was tight and smooth and she ran her hands over his chest lightly before he grabbed her hands in his. He pulled her behind him and made the short trip to his bedroom. As she had imagined, the room with the marbled bathroom was his. He stopped in front of the bed and let her go.

"Get on the bed... and then lay on your back." He said it and moved to the other side of the room to finish removing his clothes.

When she was done, she felt her heart beating out of her chest. She was laying here like a sacrifice to him. She had a need to be that for him. Whatever made him this way, whatever drove him, she didn't know. She only wanted to make him feel better, and in turn make herself feel better. He moved towards her and she lay still. She expected to see a sinister smile play across his face, but the one he had was a concerned one instead. He moved easily onto the bed, above her. Instead of ravishing her as she expected, he pulled her closer to him and held her. The action was a simple one, but necessary. She closed her eyes and felt her body relax in the warm strength of his arms. She needed this, the security of it. It wouldn't be long before even this moment was a memory, and she wanted to enjoy it for as long as she could. They lay that way for a while, his hands slowly moving along her arms and hips. His movements were not sexual but more loving than anything.

He raised above her slightly to look at her. She was beautiful and she was laying in his bed, something that never happened. He always made a point of being with women someplace else, never here. She was special, he knew it from the beginning, but what he was feeling now was new for him.

"Do you want to talk about it Sierra?" He played with an auburn curl as he looked down at her. She reached up and put her hand on his cheek.

"No, I don't want to talk, A.J. I just want to feel safe, and wanted." Their eyes made contact and the mood shifted dramatically.

"Are you sure?" He took the time to make the extra effort before he touched her like that. He was fighting his instincts already, trying to be there and trying to make her feel safe. If she opened that door on her own, welcoming him in, it would take very little before he gave her everything once more.

"Yes, I'm sure... love me, A.J."

He needed no further invitation and his mouth found her full and red lips eagerly. His actions were focused and specific, even he felt the trembling need building within. Her hair was spread across the pillow like a flame, and the lingerie he had sent fit her like a glove. He held his focus on her mouth, kissing her and feeding off of her lips until they were bruised. She touched him back, running her fingers down his back and in his hair as he kissed on her. He moved his hands down her shoulders and chest casually licking and nipping through the lace of her clothing. He nipped the skin on her belly, all the while his hands were freeing her upper body from the confinement of the outfit. He used his hands to cup and love on her until he made his way back up. It was almost painful when he would move the heat of his mouth off of her skin and move to another area. She reveled in the feel of him on her and the patterns his mouth made on her flesh... Her body was on fire. Her hands pulling his head up and back to her waiting mouth. He did as she asked and gave her a passionate kiss, drinking from her mouth. She wanted this, wanted him more now than ever. Only he could make her forget their pain and the worry of what life had in store for her. Only he could take her someplace else.

He made a leisurely trail down the rest of her body, leaving no area untouched by him. Suddenly stood back to look at her naked form splayed across the bed. She felt no shame in it, in this moment she belonged to him.

"You are mine, Sierra, do you understand that... only mine." She nodded to him and he smiled at her before making a trail up her thighs with his mouth. Soon it was too much, the way he touched her, the way he loved her. She wanted to be in this moment for as long as possible

He moved above her and she felt the joining of their body's like a tidal wave. He felt the heat of her envelop him and he stopped, waiting and feeling her. She was more than any women he had ever known and he knew he was forever changed. There was and urgency to hold her, to love her. He moved slowly, savoring every second of it, she was lost in it, just as he, he had thrown back and her eyes were glazed over from his lover. She looked at him now as he moved and he never broke stride once as he laid his chest against hers and kissed her deeply. She moaned loudly, driving him more and he his pace became quicker, more demanding. Both unwilling to let go of what they felt they had moved frantically exploring and enjoying the other. She was lost in a swirling of color and heat. She felt the familiar stirrings deep down and her eyes fluttered open and she looked at him.

Her reaction was stronger than any she'd ever had before. It ripped through her and she felt it shoot through even her fingers and toes. She yelled out his name as it happened and something about that pushed him over the edge as well. He grabbed her face and leaned down over her as he found release inside her. They lay that way for a long time, both feeling and thinking. Neither of them wanting to move. She drifted off to sleep at some point and knew she was safe.

He woke up before she did and stood looking at her. She was curled on her side, oblivious to the fact she was being watched. He was lost and confused at himself. Last night he had broken more than one of his own rules. He had never been so careless with anyone. She could be pregnant from what they had done. Thinking it brought up images of what their child would look like and the warm feeling spread through him and he swore inwardly to himself. What the hell was wrong with him? He knew before he even admitted it to himself, he wanted her, wanted to be with her. She was moving, but there was no way he would allow it now. She was in his bed, and in his heart. He was all over the place with her. One minute he wanted to protect her and the next, he wanted to scold her because she was so stubborn. He wasn't sure what he would do now. He padded his way back into the living room and decided to start plating food. She would be up soon and they had to talk. This time not laying in a bed, or nothing would ever get discussed. He picked up her bag from the floor and when he did, he found a notepad with something scratched on it.

When finally she woke up, she knew he was gone. She moved to the shower and washed the lovemaking off of her from before. She felt him come in before he said a word. He waited, a hooded look to his eyes

"Why didn't you tell me someone was trying to hurt you, Sierra?" He picked up the soap from the dish and lathered up the sponge she was holding. He started with her shoulders, making lazy circles as he washed her.

"Why would I tell you, A.J.?" she managed to get the words out despite the sensations he was creating with the sponge. He moved the sponge lower lathering her as he went.

"I told you that you belong to me, Sierra, and that means everything. If anyone tries to hurt you, that is my business too."

She bit her lip to keep from giving him the satisfaction of knowing what he was doing to her again. When he was around, she lost all control of her body. He turned off the water and dried her off helping her get dressed in a shirt of his. She had to admit to herself she was left wanting more. They walked into the kitchen where the food was still warm and he played it for them all the while watching her. She looked at him, she had never seen him this way. He was wearing sweats and a t-shirt. Gone was the tailored suit and tie, even his hair was a ruffled mess, and she was lost.

"Sierra, hello." He was waving his hand in front of her and she snapped back to the present.

Finally, he asked.

"This guy, is his name Brandon? Don't lie to me."

"Yes, but how did you know that A.J.?" she stopped eating and looked at him.

"I had someone look into the situation this afternoon after you left. They are coming by tonight with an update. I'd rather you know now, than to be upset later." He took a long drink. "Then there is this." He slapped the notepad from her bag on the table and she went pale.

"A.J. it's not what you think." She took a step backwards as he turned to look at her, anger apparent on his face.

"Really, it's not?" he read from the list. "Get him to fall for me pros, Jacobs meds, great sex... thanks for that one by the way, not being scared." He looked at her with her head down now. "Cons of getting him to fall for me. He is a playboy, great sex and the best one... incapable of love." He threw the pad on the table in her direction.

"I write a lot about what's in my head, A.J. that's all. I knew better and I wouldn't even try...."

He cut her off "Really, you wouldn't try? When you first came in the office tonight you were handsy then, were you not trying?" He was bitter and upset.

"Well, yes, but I knew it was wrong and I couldn't... I'm not stupid, A.J., I knew better than to even consider it." She grabbed the pad up from the table and walked over to face him. "Exactly what part are you mad about, A.J.? The fact that I said the sex was great or the fact that someone else considered turning your own games against you, which is it?" She spun around but he was there in an instant. He was inches away from her face and his eyes softened.

"You're right, everything on that list is right, so I guess you win. I brought you here to protect you, I'm not as horrible as you think."

She was angry. "You have no right to get involved, A.J., he is misguided and yes, he scares me but this is not your problem to look into." She stood quickly and made her way back to the bedroom they had shared only hours before. She looked around gathering her clothes, but her bag was gone. She was on her way back into the kitchen where he still sat eating and she stopped. He didn't move, only continued to eat.

When she headed towards the door he finally spoke to her. "Sierra, don't."

He said it with such deep intent, it made her freeze in her tracks. He was there in an instant. He stood in front of her, between her and the door. He reached up and gently brushed her hair away from her face. She saw something different in his eyes then, something she couldn't place. He reached up and cupped her face in his hand and kissed her gently. Suddenly there was a knock on the door. He stood back and opened it, letting in a man in a dark coat. He grabbed her hand in his and brought her with him to the bar where the man could share his findings.

"This man, Brandon Baker, he isn't who he says he is. We checked your car and spoke with some people in the neighborhood and we are pretty sure he is the one who did it. That isn't the real problem."

Sierra felt the dread welling up inside her as he continued to speak. Whatever it was, it couldn't be good.

"His description fits a suspect that is wanted in the disappearance of a woman in Montana. Apparently he was too overwhelming and suddenly she went missing. The guy they are looking for is Richard Carson, but I was able to track his entrance into town around the same time Mr. Randolph disappeared from Montana. I think it's worth looking into."

A.J. spoke first. "Thank you Darius. I'll be in touch, but I definitely want this handled, and quickly."

Sierra was in shock, the tears streaming down her face. She dated Brandon for two years before he started to act this way, at any moment she could have been hurt. She had to get home where she was safe, where everyone was safe. She turned around and suddenly he was there. He pulled her into his arms and she let it all go, the tears and her heartache, for the time spent with someone who could hurt her. She pulled away and wiped her face.

"I have to go home, to my father's." She headed back to the door.

"No, it's not safe Sierra, stay here, with me." He stood there and she glanced between the door and him. She wasn't sure what to do.

"Then what, A.J., stay here until morning and then be scared to even go home to get my things?" She slumped down to the couch. She started to put on her shoes and he watched her helplessly.

She suddenly leaned forward and he knew she was crying. Instinctively he moved towards her, gathering her up in his arms. He knew she wouldn't put up a fight and he carried her to his room and his bed. She silently let the tears go unchecked down her face. She didn't want to fight the emotions anymore, she just needed to let it all go. She didn't say a word as he undressed her and tucked her into the bed. He followed suit and spooned in behind her, pulling her into his arms. She rolled over and let him wrap her up, laying her head on his chest and cried until she was asleep. He looked down at her, gently stroking her hair and enjoying the heat of her body against this. There was a simple pleasure in this, something with no sexual bearing, he was in uncharted territory. He was losing himself with her, his focus had shifted to loving her, and protecting her. She was determined to run, but he wouldn't let her, she just needed to realize what she felt back to him too. It would take some patience, but he would show her, he had too, or lose herself in the process.

Sierra was aware of everything around her. She had been lying there, thinking about what was to come for a long time. He was there, beside her. It felt like the most natural thing in the world to be here with him like this. She was in love with him, but he would never know it. He was a playboy and that would never change. She slid away from him slightly and in his sleep, he pulled her back to him. With a sigh, she let herself feel for a while longer. The next time she woke he was gone. She had planned to try and leave quietly, not disturbing him. It was no longer an option since he was in the kitchen. She threw on his shirt and walked quietly into the room and watched him. He was humming to himself and stirring something on the stove. He finally noticed her there and he froze.

Standing there, in his shirt and her hair a tangled mess she was the most beautiful thing he had ever seen. She was watching him with a half-smile and he could almost feel his heart beating out of his chest. He looked like an idiot standing there staring and he shook his head slightly to get it together.

> "I see you're up, sleepyhead, coffee is ready and breakfast will be in a moment." He turned back to what he was doing and she watched the muscles in his back flex as he worked. There was something sexy about a man cooking and she smiled despite the knowing fear in her stomach about the day to come.

> "Thank you, I have to go soon, but I'll stay and eat. It looks heavenly!" He delivered her eggs and bacon with pancakes and she sat back overwhelmed by the food on her plate.

> "Sorry, I have a rather big appetite for breakfast food." He shrugged and joined her at the bar.

They ate in silence, neither wanting to broach the topic at hand. They would smile from time to time, but it was a quiet affair. Once everything had been cleared, she couldn't avoid it any longer.

> "A.J., I can't thank you enough, for everything you did for me last night." She gave him a smile as she wound her mass of hair up into a bun.

> He watched the woman he loved become the woman he was afraid of, all business and stern.

"Sierra, we need to talk. I don't want you to move, especially with that guy still running loose. I don't trust the situation." He couldn't say the words he was really feeling, not yet, it was still too new.

"It's not just about that, A.J. There is much more to it. My father needs me."

He stood. "I asked you if your family needed you, if they were in trouble." He frowned at her.

"I know you did, and I just didn't want to add to the situation, I'm sorry." She slipped out of his shirt and changed back into her clothes. He took a steadying breath as he watched her naked form move and sway with her movements, this was damn near killing him.

He moved towards her and upped her chin in his hand. "Tell me Sierra, please talk to me."

She looked at his expression and knew he was being sincere. With a sigh she settled back into the barstool. "My father is taking out a loan on the house today and I have to go sign paperwork with him. It's a legal issue more than anything. When my mother died I was given executor over the estate because my father didn't want to have any part of it, he was devastated when she died."

"Why does he need to take out a loan on the house?" He frowned.

"It doesn't matter why A.J., you asked what I had to do, and I told you." Her eyes were flashing at him and he knew she was angry. As she went into the bathroom to fix her face, he took matters into his own hands, that's how she found him when she came back out.

"Oh yes, I completely understand, yes, Mr. Ford. I'm happy to help, really, that won't be necessary. Give him a hug from us. Okay, bye."

She was standing there with her hands on her hips, fuming. When he hung up he knew there would be hell before she even began.

"Was that my father? My father, A.J., really you went to him? Since when do you have his number anyway!" she was pacing and he watched her, amused.

"Since lunch, we exchanged numbers. To be fair Sierra, I asked you first, but you wouldn't tell me anything, so I asked him." He moved towards her and she backed away and he frowned.

"You have no right always butting into everything I do, A.J., you shouldn't have called him, now he is going to worry. I dumped all of our problems at his feet, he is going to be worried. I won't be there today to handle the business side of the situation. What exactly did he tell you?" She stopped pacing and peered at him.

"You don't need to go sign the paperwork, he decided not to take a loan out on the house. We talked about Jacob, of course." He waited for the next round of anger to start.

"What did you do, A.J., what did you do?" She whispered it and he was even more concerned. He could handle her fire, but this was new.

"I took care of it, I offered to pay for Jacobs's medicine. You could have talked to me about it, Sierra. I would have helped." She flashed him a look and he felt it like a slap.

"Is that how it is now, A.J.? I stay here, we are... together and now you swoop in and fix my problems?" She waited.

He was angry now. "Hours ago Sierra, I confronted you about planning the same thing. You contemplated it and now you're throwing it at me when the fact of the matter is I'm not doing it for any other reason than the fact that I love you." He was yelling now and he watched her face shift and turn red. He ran a hand through his hair and walked to the bedroom to cool off. He knew she couldn't go anywhere and he needed to breathe, she made him crazy and he had just said he loved her. He felt her enter the room before he even saw her. He turned around to see her crying and he immediately sobered.

"Don't do that Sierra, I can't handle you crying. I am sorry, for whatever I did wrong. It doesn't change the way I feel."

"I love you too, A.J. I think I always have." She wiped her face.

He felt his heart soar as he took the few short strides to her and he gathered her up in his arms.

"Arnold." He kissed her and held her close.

"What?" She looked back up at him puzzled.

"That's what the A stands for. It's Arnold, and I thought since we love each other you should know." He gave her a smile.

"What about the J?" She waited.

"Oh no, one name at a time, you have to earn the other one." She giggled and he kissed her again.

******

Second Chance Romance

Cocky Justin dumped plus size Jodi after he hooked up with a younger, thinner, more attractive woman. While Jodi tried moving on with her life, she couldn't shake the paralyzing depression she felt.

She craved Justin's love more than ever, even though it had been three years since he'd left her. She begged him to take her back but this only turned him off more.

Jodi met charismatic Justin when he came into the hair salon where she worked. She fell in love with him at first sight even though she found him arrogant, cocky and brazen. Everything about him was thrilling to her. He was a champion polo player who belonged to an exclusive country club and he traveled all over the world.

Jodi grew up poor, and while she did well in high school, she was unable to attend college because of financial constraints and responsibilities at home. After her father got fired from his job, Jodi had to work full-time to help pay the bills.

Justin was 12 years older than Jodi, although he acted much younger. She found his friends to be boring, stodgy, and arrogant. Despite her disdain for his friends, she quickly fell in love with him. He treated her like a queen, and even offered to pay for her to go back to college. At first, they were blissfully happy.

The couple soon settled into a mundane dating routine, and although Jodi was still jubilant about their relationship, she sensed that Justin was becoming restless and bored with her. He seemed irritated and distant, and even stopped coming home after work. When he began hurling cruel comments to her, she felt hopeless and vulnerable.

Most of Justin's family members liked Jodi but his mother never warmed up to her. She never thought that Jodi was pretty or smart enough for her son, but remained cordial to her.

Justin's mother, Caroline, on more than one occasion, tried introducing her son to various women. These women were all professionals, and a few were lawyers, just like her son.

Justin's father, Peter, also an attorney, stayed out of his wife's shameless matchmaking schemes. He was in his own little world, with a mistress of his own and a huge drinking problem.

Justin didn't invite Jodi to his grandmother's birthday party, and when he arrived, he was greeted at the door by one of the most beautiful women he'd ever seen. He never saw her before, and wondered who she was there with. Little did he know, his mother invited her in an attempt to get him interested in someone other than Jodi.

Her plan worked. Justin and the other women, whose name was Christine, hit it off almost instantly. He couldn't stop looking at her, and was intrigued by her New York accent.

Christine worked as an entertainment attorney, who represented a number of big name sports and music personalities. She even invited Justine to a sporting event which had been sold out for weeks.

Even though Justin had no intentions of breaking up with Jodi, he could no longer ignore his feelings for Christine. They soon started having lunch dates at 5 star hotels, and even managed to plan a getaway weekend to the Poconos.

When Justin started becoming increasingly distant from Jodi, she started to suspect the worst. By this time, Christine was pressuring Justine for a commitment. Although they've only been seeing each other for about a month, their relationship was growing more and more intense.

The sex was amazing, and Justin never experienced anything like it before. Christine was willing to try new things in bed, and seemed to want sex multiple times a day. Jodi, by contrast, was rather modest, and her sexual appetite was diminished by her escalating depression, and the side effects from the medication she was taking.

As the months passed, Jodi was getting ready to go to Florida for a hair show. She and Justin were drifting further and further apart, but they still managed to maintain a dim spark of excitement between them. On the evening before she was schedule to leave for her trip, Jodi and Justin went out for a romantic dinner, and then came home and spent the next three hours making love.

After their love fest, Justin turned over and went to sleep. Jodi, the eternal romantic, want to cuddle, but Justin rebuffed her advances. The next morning, Justin drove Jodi to the airport, and he couldn't help but feel profound relief. He would now be able to spend the next week with his new "friend," Christine, and called her as soon as Jodi boarded the plane.

For almost the entire week that Jodi was on her business trip, Justin stayed with Christine at her downtown apartment. The couple enjoyed cooking dinner together and waking up next to each other. Justin didn't know how he would tell Jodi that he no longer loved her, and he even wished that she would stay in Florida for the long-term.

He was not responsive to her text messages, and only took her phone calls sporadically during that entire week. The week flew by quickly, and before he knew it, Justin found himself at the airport once again, but only this time, he was picking Jodi up. She was elated to see him, but he cringed when they hugged.

Jodi sensed that something was wrong, and was starting to worry. Justin told her that he was tired because he spent the entire week working on a brief for an upcoming legal case.

The couple trudged through the holidays together, but as Valentine's Day approached, Justin could no longer suppress he desire to be with Christine. Although he knew that Valentine's week was not the most appropriate time to break up with Jodi, he felt it was necessary, because he wanted to spend Valentine's Day with Christine.

He didn't bother with formalities, and simply blurted it out. He told Jodi that he was no longer happy with her, but didn't volunteer any information about his other woman. He further explained that he just needed time to be "by himself," and that "maybe" he would come to his senses and come back home to be with her. After Jodi pressed him for answers, he finally came clean about Christine.

After hearing the news, Jodi broke down, and didn't think she would be able to function at work the next day. Of course, Justin told her that he didn't mean for it to happen, but when he met Christine, an instant connection was made. He didn't really want to divulge so much information about how he felt about Christine, but he felt that unless he "drove his point home," Jodi wouldn't take him seriously.

Jodi was blindsided by the breakup. She tried to keep busy with work and going out with friends, but she couldn't shake the despair she felt. Although she was asked out on dates, she always declined.

In Jodi's eyes, nobody would ever hold a candle to Justin, and she had no desire to date anyone because she knew it would never progress into anything further. In the meantime, Justin and Christine were seen around town at various restaurants and social events.

On one occasion, Jodi caught a glimpse of the couple getting out of a cab. This almost pushed her over the edge, but she managed to hold onto her dignity. After three years passed, Jodi's feelings for Justin were still as intense as they were when they first started dated. Justin's feelings for Jodi, on the other hand, were almost non-existent. Sure, he had fond memories of their time together, but never really felt as though Jodi was his soul mate.

Jodi eventually started seeing a counselor because she was not bouncing back from the breakup. Her sleep pattern was disrupted, her diet was poor, and she stopped socializing altogether. The only social stimulation she got was when she went to work, and even there, her social interactions were severely limited.

The counselor was worried for his patient's safety, and feared that she was spiraling into a deep, dark depression. Jodi was eventually referred to a psychiatrist, who adjusted her medication and sent her on her way. When the medication kicked in after a few weeks, Jodi's mood brightened, and she started considering dating again.

Jodi met a nice guy at the gym, and when he asked her out for coffee, she felt flattered. Like Justin, Brandon was older, distinguished and well-educated. Their coffee date was pleasant, but according to Jodi, there was no spark.

When Brandon asked her out for dinner, Jodi hesitated, but decided to give him another chance. She was very critical of other men, but hoped that she would once again, find love. Brandon took Jodi to dinner and a play, and as the date was coming to a close, Brandon leaned in for a kiss.

Jodi had no intentions of kissing him, and in fact, she had no intentions of ever seeing him again. All she could think about was Justin. Three years have passed, and still, her love was as strong as ever. Jodi's co-workers were worried about her, and when she had too much to drink one night and drunk dialed Justin, they really became concerned. Fortunately, she hung up before he answered the phone, but her number showed up on his caller ID.

Justin was curious to find out what Jodi wanted. His relationship with Christine was starting to cool, and lately, he started thinking about how much Jodi loved him when they were together. He hesitated at first, but after a couple days, Justin returned Jodi's call.

You could have knocked her over with a feather when she saw Justin's number come up on her caller ID. She was shaking as she answered the phone, and as soon as she heard his voice, she broke down sobbing.

Something stirred in Justin's heart, because he too, felt tears welling up in his eyes. Their phone call was brief, and in fact, it lasted only seconds, because Christine walked into the room just as Jodi answered. Justin took this as a sign.

Jodi knew that Justin still felt a connection to her. She quickly put that phone call out of her mind, and tried to focus on her job. She went on a few more dates, and much to her surprise, Jodi found a guy with whom she clicked with.

Her friend introduced her to an accountant who was from the same town that she was from. In fact, they lived within a few blocks of each other when they were teenagers, but they went to different schools. He went to a private, all-boys school, and Jodi went to a public school.

At first, the relationship progressed slowly, but after a few months, Jodi started developing strong feelings for her new friend, whose name was Nathan. He took Jodi to meet his family in New Hampshire, and they absolutely loved her. Unlike Justin's mother, Caroline, Nathan's mother, Kerry, felt that they were the perfect couple.

As their relationship grew stronger, Jodi's feelings for Justin were becoming distant memories. In fact, days went by where she didn't even think about Justin at all. Justin, on the other hand, couldn't get Jodi out of his mind. His relationship with Christine was hanging by a thread, and he yearned for the relationship he once shared with Jodi.

He was starting to realize that breaking up with her was a mistake, and he hoped that she was not involved with another man. Justin finally raised enough courage to call Jodi back, and when she answered, his heart stopped. He almost hung up, but was able to whisper out a weak, "Hi Jodi, how are you?" Jodi was gracious and warm, and replied, "Hi, Justin, it's nice to hear from you."

The conversation was strained and awkward, but in Justin's mind, the ice had been broken. He was certain that he could get back into Jodi's good graces once again, so that they could pick up where they left off. Their conversation consisted solely of small talk, and neither one asked about the other's personal life.

Jodi almost felt sick to her stomach when she heard Justin's voice, because it brought back the painful memories of their breakup. She was grateful that she had Nathan, because he filled the void that Justin left. When she told Nathan that Justin called, he became suspicious.

Why, he thought, would Justin call Jodi, out of the blue, after three years apart. Did Jodi initiate the first call, he wondered? Jodi finally confessed to Nathan that she did, indeed, "drunk dial" Justin days before.

It seemed that now, the tables were turned. Justin was the one who was pining away for Jodi, while Jodi, on the other hand, was blissfully "in like" with someone else. It never occurred to Justin that Jodi would move on and start a new life with someone else. He also felt that Jodi was his "ace in the hole," in case his relationship with Christine didn't work out. Would he and Jodi ever reconcile, he wondered?

Even though Jodi was happy with Nathan, she couldn't get Justin out of her mind, and wanted to connect with him again, just to find out more about his relationship status with Christine.

Jodi felt a twinge of guilt for thinking about calling Justin because Nathan had been so good to her. She didn't want to be shady or go behind his back, so she talked to him about her intentions.

Jodi felt that she needed to get Justin out of her system once and for all before she would be able to move forward with her relationship with Nathan. A total commitment to Nathan was out of the question, in Jodi's mind, unless she was completely over Justin.

Nathan agreed that Jodi needed to get Justin out of her system before they could take the next step in their relationship, so he encouraged Jodi to make the phone call. Feeling better now that she confessed her feelings to Nathan about Justin, Jodi picked up the phone and dialed his number.

He answered on the first ring, and couldn't believe his good fortune that Jodi was calling him. "I want to see you," Jodi said, as soon as Justin answered the phone.

Justin was shocked, but elated. By this time, he and Christine were barely speaking, and she was spending more and more time away from the apartment that they shared since the beginning of their relationship.

Jodi and Justin planned to go out for dinner so that could talk. Both were excited, anxious, but uncertain about a future together. When Jodi saw Justin for the first time in three years, she was surprised that her heart wasn't racing, and that she did not have butterflies in her stomach.

Although it was nice to see Justin, that intense spark of passion and love was not there. Justin, on the other hand, could barely contain his emotions, and started to cry when they hugged.

He apologized to Jodi for hurting her, but she was unfazed. The cold and uncaring way that he "dumped" Jodi always bothered him, but he never had the opportunity to tell Jodi how he felt. They talked about hidi relationship with Christine, and how it started out so intensely, but then, over time, seemed to have burned itself out.

Jodi listened quietly as Justin spoke about how Christine was a workaholic, and how she never cooked a meal for him in three years. Not only didn't she cook, she never cleaned either. Justin finally hired a cleaning service to come in twice a month to tidy up, but he wished that Christine was a little more domesticated. She wasn't into the "housewife" thing, and she certainly didn't have any maternal instincts either. Jodi couldn't help but feel a twinge of satisfaction while Justin was droning on about his faltering relationship with Christine.

Justin was the type of guy who enjoyed home-cooked meals, who liked a clean home, and who wanted to start a family someday. Jodi wanted to start a family too, but it was becoming more apparent to Jodi, that instead of wanting to start a family with Justin, she wanted to start one with Nathan.

Throughout the entire dinner, Justin talked about himself and his relationship with Christine. He didn't ask Jodi what was going on in her life until it was almost time for them to leave.

Justin was certain that Jodi had been waiting around for him to come back all this time, and was profoundly disappointed when Jodi told him that she had met someone else. What made Justin feel even worse was when Jodi told him that she was falling in love with Nathan. Justin asked, "how could you have fallen out of love with me?" Jodi replied, " It took a long time, but I finally found someone who appreciates me, embraces me for who I am, and whose family loves me." On one hand, Justin was happy for Jodi, but on the other hand, he was jealous, hurt and angry.

How could he have let Jodi go? He knew what a great woman she was, but he let his mother's silly opinion of Jodi get in the way. Justin now realizes that Jodi was the "one that got away," and his hopes of finding his one true love have been dashed.

As their dinner date was ending, Justin felt that he had lost Jodi forever. He decided to swallow his pride and beg Jodi for another chance. He realized the error of his ways, and vowed that if she would give him another chance, he would do everything in his power to make her the happiest women alive.

Although tempting, Jodi gently declined. Her feelings for Justin had changed, and she knew that she would never be able to love him like she once had. Justin wouldn't let up on his request for another chance, and Jodi, who kept politely turning him down, was getting increasingly aggravated by his persistence. Jodi once thought that the sun rose and set on Justin, but now, she was beginning to see his true colors emerge.

Justin had always been on the arrogant side, and was accustomed to getting his way all the time. He was spoiled as a child, and always seemed to have the upper hand when it came to relationships. If he didn't get what he wanted, he became pushy, overbearing and selfish.

Justin was sure that if he kissed Jodi, that old spark would re-ignite in her soul. Not only did Jodi turn away from Justin's attempt at a kiss, she was repelled by it. He no longer had the same effect on her, and in fact, she wished that she could have snapped her fingers to bring her back home to Nathan. She felt safe with him because he was so genuine and kind. There was not an arrogant or selfish bone in his body.

Jodi always lived on the edge with Justin, and always questioned his feelings for her. She knows that Nathan is in love with her, and only her. He is not on the lookout for someone better, or for someone who is on the same level as he is educationally. Even though Jodi doesn't have a college education, she is extremely bright, quick witted, wise and perceptive. Qualities that Justin never saw in her.

He criticized Jodi because of the way she spoke and because she never attended college. He wanted to pay for her college education so that she could "better herself," however, Jodi believes that he only wanted her to go to college because he was concerned that she wasn't "scholarly" enough, and that it didn't look good for him to be with an "uneducated" woman.

Just to make sure that Justin was completely out of her system, Jodi relented, and kissed him. The kiss soon became more intense, and Jodi could sense that Justin was getting overly enthusiastic. Since she wasn't feeling the same way, she retreated. She now knew, for sure, that Justin wasn't the man for her. When she kissed Nathan, passion stirred inside her, but when she kissed Justin, she felt nothing.

Although Jodi felt guilty about kissing Justin because she knew it would hurt Nathan, she just had to know for sure if the excitement, love and passion were still there. They were for Justin, but not for Jodi. It was then and there, that she decided to say good-bye, once and for all. Jodi would never turn back, and would finally close that chapter in her life.

After a year had gone by, Jody and Nathan started planning their wedding. They were now totally committed to each other, and were living together. Jodi quit her job as a hair stylist, and was now working for Nathan. This allowed them to spend all day together, which they cherished. Some couples enjoy the time they spend away from each other while they are both at their respective jobs, but for Jodi and Nathan, working together in the same office works well for them. In addition to being soul mates, they are best friends, and can let their respective guards down when they are together.

Although Nathan is technically Jodi's boss, he never plays that card. He is also careful, however, to never show favoritism to Jodi in front of his other employees. He treats everyone with respect, and no one is treated better than anyone else. Many of Nathan's employees have been with his for years, which is a true testament to his character. Jodi is proud to be his life partner, both personally and professionally.

Jodi was getting excited for her wedding, and before the big day, members of her bridal party gave her a bachelorette party. Jodi almost forgot what it was like to have a good time with her friends, because the last time they all went out together, Jodi was in a funk over Justin.

She is grateful that her friends saw her through her ordeal, and is honored to have them be a part of her wedding day. The celebration started off at a neighborhood bar where the ladies indulged in a few tropical drinks, then it was off to Jodi's favorite restaurant. The night was exciting and fun, and Jodi couldn't remember when she had such a fun time with her friends.

The merriment came to a screeching halt in the blink of an eye, however. While the ladies were enjoying their dinner and each other's company, a familiar figure walked through the door. It was none other than Justin. He was accompanied by an older woman, who Jodi later recognized as his mother, Caroline. The two looked solemn as they were seated at their table, and barely spoke to one another while they dined.

Justin and his mother hadn't yet noticed that Jodi was at the restaurant, and Jodi wanted it to stay that way. She didn't want anything to ruin her special evening, but when she had to go to the bathroom, she wondered how she'd sneak past their table without her cover being blown.

After thinking about it, she realized that she didn't care if they saw her or not. She didn't owe either one of them anything and didn't even feel obligated to greet them. Jodi and her entourage made a beeline for the bathroom, but not before Justin's mother noticed them. "Isn't that Jodi?" she asked.

Justin was stunned and took this as another opportunity to try and win her back. It's fate, he thought. Yes, it was fate, but not in the way that Justin had hoped for. He stalked the bathroom door and waiting for Jodi to come out. When she did, he greeted her with a hug. Jodi tried to be personable, but again, she couldn't hide her disdain for Justin.

Jodi and Justin ended up having a brief conversation. Jodi was more than happy to tell Justin about her impending nuptials to Nathan. She then learned why Justin and his mother looked so stone-faced when they walked into the restaurant.

It turned out that Justin was the one who was now battling severe depression ever since Jodi didn't return his affections the last time they had dinner together. In fact, his depression got so bad that he had to give up his law practice and move in with his mother.

This was the first night he had been out in public in months. His relationship with Christine had long since fell apart, and he was having a hard time re-building his life. Jodi felt bad for Justin, and now wondered if his mother felt any remorse for sticking her nose in their business by setting him up with Christine.

Jodi and Nathan were married in a beautiful ceremony, and now have an adorable baby girl. Justin is still living with his mother, and has let his law license expire. He did get a job working as a handyman in the neighborhood, however, and Jodi has since shown pity on him and hired him to install a white picket fence around her and Nathan's sprawling new home. Karma at its best...

******

About the Author

J.L. Ryan is a bestselling romance author who loves writing billionaire romance, bad boy romance, BBW romance, slow burn romance, angsty romance, and second chance romance books. She's been an author for the past 20 years, and has conducted literary workshops to help aspiring authors improve their writing skills. She likes to attend author and publishing conventions, workshops, and seminars, where many of her books are featured. Here are some of the many genres, categories, and characters she enjoys writing about: Billionaire Romance Bad Boy Romance Plus Size Romance A Good Billionaire Love Story Or Series Playboy Romance Wealthy Romance Hot Romance Novels Steamy Romance Novels Second Chance Romance Alpha Male Romance Older Man Younger Woman Romance Billionaire Obsession Billionaire Bachelors Rich Romance Rich Man Poor Woman HEA HEA Romance Small Town Romance Return To Hometown Romance Slow Burn Romance Angsty Romance Boss Romance Office Romance Lawyer Romance Medical Romance Bad Boy Alphas

Billionaire Bad Boy Romance Bad Boy Rebels Sweet Romance Inspirational Romance Clean And Wholesome Romance Contemporary Romance Contemporary Women's Fiction And More...

www.ingramcontent.com/pod-product-compliance
Lightning Source LLC
Chambersburg PA
CBHW020909180626
46816CB00007BA/2315